AGAINST NATURE

&

Other Abominations

Books by Melinda Selmys:

Fiction

Eros & Thanatos

Tales from Grandma Bo's Cottage

Against Nature & Other Abominations

Non Fiction

Sexual Authenticity: An Intimate Reflection on Homosexuality and Catholicism

Sexual Authenticity: More Reflections

Slave of Two Masters

AGAINST NATURE

&

Other Abominations

MELINDA SELMYS

vulgata

ISBN 978-0991909896

"Lubyanka" first appeared in Vol. III, No. 2 of *Hungur Magazine* in 2008

"Schrödinger's Zombie" first appeared in *Tales of the Zombie War*

"The Faery Cry" first appeared in Volume 3 Issue 2 of *Non-Euclidean Café* in 2008

"Rite of Atonement" first appeared on *Pseudopod* in November, 2007

"Who's Afraid of the Little Red Hood?" first appeared in *SpeckLit*

"Achilles in Purple" first appeared in the September issue of *Byzarium* in 2007

"The Dying Place" First appeared in the anthology *Love, Time, Space & Magic*

"Pedro's Treasure" first appeared in issue XVII of *Vulgata Magazine* in October, 2007

"A Very Long Bereavement" first appeared in *SpeckLit*

for Eve

CONTENTS

• • • • •

CATASTROPHIC BEAUTY

It was the moment that every artist fears, when he steps back from his work and sees for the first time what he has wrought. It was an object of catastrophic beauty. A little lopsided, perhaps, but the asymmetry (by no means intentional) somehow added to its wretched charm.

A great pendulous tongue hung from its mouth almost down to its knees, its pitted surface blackened with a mixture of ash, oil and bitumen. The boils that had erupted on its palsied arms almost seemed to twinkle like jewels, so perfectly had he captured the curious pearlescent scabs that gave the Ruby Plague its name. One eye was widened, the other sewn shut with the cakey pus that accumulated around the eyes of the dying. It was perfect. Larger than life, disproportionate, all of its limbs the wrong size, misshapen and ghastly. He was calling it "Exorcism of Memory."

Down in the courtyard, a bell tolled. It was exactly on time according to the clock on the wall — but the clock had stopped ticking nearly a year ago and Morgan had not considered it important enough to waste batteries. People kept talking about how the power was going to be restored, and every so often there would be a little hiccup, a couple of minutes of powerful illumination causing the city to shine out like a beacon on the hillside. The longest had lasted for nearly an hour before the grid had shaken its weary carcass and the streetlights had lost their hope. There were a couple of survivors in the building next door who seemed to look upon these events as pools in a desert. Morgan always thought there was something hideous and pathetic about it, like when the body of a fish continues to flop after being skinned and filleted.

Extinguishing the candle that he had used to improve the rather dismal lighting situation in his apartment, he rushed downstairs. No elevators. It had occurred to him several times that he might move to one of the vacant apartments on the ground floor but everyone needed their little observances to keep them sane, and one of his was the refusal to expand his small kingdom. He pillaged, obviously. Everybody pillaged. But he didn't bathe in other people's bathtubs, or sleep in their beds, or sit on their couches staring blankly at his reflection in their dead television screens. The rest of the building was permitted to remain as a kind of tomb which he, in desperation, occasionally robbed. Only the storage space in the basement and the superintendent's office on the main floor had actually been appropriated.

Third in line. It wasn't bad timing. He'd painted a family portrait for the milk-man shortly after it had become apparent that it was important to cultivate a sense of obligation in others. In return, the milk deliveries were made just under Morgan's window.

"What do you come for?" the man intoned. The shadow-look had been growing in his eyes over the past three months. It was probable at this point that he didn't even remember about the portrait, or about the glass of wine that they had shared, but he continued to appear here out of habit and that was good enough.

"I come for milk."

"And do you serve?"

"If necessary."

A momentary look of confusion crossed the man's face. He was definitely drifting. Once upon a time he would have smiled and thumbed his nose. "It is necessary," he said slowly.

"Then I suppose I must."

The bottle was produced and handed over with reluctance. Clearly Morgan's credit was starting to run out. The idol would fix all that. "Thank you," he said. With a small bow he ceded the line to the next supplicant. His own conversation with the milk-man was repeated verbatim, except that instead of saying "if necessary" the weathered looking woman in the desperate silk-handkerchief heaved a troubled sigh and replied, "All must serve."

It was a terrible drink, "milk" only by virtue of the fact that it was cloudy and smelled faintly of a barnyard. God knew what was in it — assuming that God still existed and had dared to look. The color was unwholesomely pink but it kept you alive. If the rumors were to be believed, it would keep you alive forever. Morgan desperately hoped that the rumors were not to be believed. Just in case, he drank as little as he could and used most of his ration to feed the tomatoes that grew in pots on the balcony. Since they had started this regimen of feeding they had taken on a slightly dusky cast and Morgan's tomato sauces had become redolent with a suggestion of fresh-spilled blood and embalming spices — not altogether an unpleasant taste, but one that contributed to the general atmosphere of gloom that had descended over the city since the Rising. On the other hand, the plants had produced a steady supply of prodigious, multi-lobed fruits and had gone on setting all throughout the winter.

He knocked back a small shot of the milk, took the rest out onto the balcony and fed the plants. Besides the tomatoes there were several hot peppers, a cucumber whose dark vines had a strangle-hold on a white-washed trellis and a frankly hellish looking rosemary whose leaves had an eerily toothy appearance. Only the tomatoes had originally been his: the rest had been saved from neighboring balconies, most of them half-dried skeletons of plants that had been restored to life by the miraculous fertilizer from which they daily drank. Morgan only hoped that they processed enough of the stuff to keep the drifting at bay. So far as he'd been able to make out, those who had their own supplies of food stayed more themselves for longer. He had a stash in the basement, of course, pillaged from the empty apartments but he used it sparingly: those who relied solely on pillage would eventually rely solely on milk when the remnants of civilization had been utterly plundered.

When he finished ministering to his flock of vegetables he returned inside and looked again at the monstrosity that he had crafted. It would have been simply hideous, should have been simply hideous. But there was something about the eyes. Behind the rheumy rims and the cloudy irises there was a hidden secret, perhaps only visible to the eyes of its creator. In the utmost extremity of its suffering it had retained its dignity. Distorted, deformed, dying and diseased. Yes, it was. But beneath that terrible exterior, a portrait of a human being.

It was a dangerous game to play and Morgan knew it. He only had to hope that the shadow which draped itself over the consciousness of the Acolytes had also dimmed their senses against the power of art. Hopefully they would be deceived into thinking that what they looked upon was a celebration of plague and death. Also hopefully — and Morgan knew that it was probably a naive and romantic hope — there would be others who remained sufficiently intact that they would look into those painted eyes and understand that they were not alone.

No one in the city knew why they had been left alive. Before the newscasts had ended they had seen the footage from other parts of the world: an entire island being lifted up on a scaly back while a thousand silver tongues flickered over the jeweled Mediterranean port and lapped up the fleeing citizens. The great darkness descending over New York like a pregnant jellyfish, her heaving bosom rising and falling in silence while from within the radios and the cell-phones went dead. A teeming multitude rising from the cracked surface of a volcanic plane, numberless swarms whose shape could not be properly discerned but whose image left the mind sick and distended. The screaming incoherence of the camera-man which continued long after the news anchor sank to the ground in front of him, clawing out her eyes with her impeccably manicured nails.

After that there had been only stories. It was said that the entire continent of Africa had been afflicted with clockwork locusts that took five hours to devour a man, and from which there was no possible shelter. Somewhere the waters themselves had been afflicted with madness and the oceans and rivers had boiled with frenzy, pipes gushed forth a torrent of churning effluent and the very fluids of the body strained and expanded until every vessel burst. In another place, the entire population had been raped to death by an indescribable monstrosity in a way so horrible that the tale-teller had fallen vomiting to the floor and fatally choked on the hideousness of his memories. Such were the stories that circulated. It was impossible to tell which were true, but there was very little reason to doubt any of them. Once the Old Ones had started to rise it had not taken them long to divide the earth according to their hungers, nor had it taken them long to reap their harvest of misery from its inhabitants.

The only real question was why so many in Morgan's district had been left alive. For a time, nearly three months after the first of the terrible gods had risen in the South Pacific, it had looked as though this little corner of the globe had been spared. Refugees had poured in. Groups had been formed for the restoration of humanity: the same groups that still struggled pitifully to restore the power, to resume postal service, to find a way of overcoming the universal scourge of infertility that afflicted the survivors. There had even been religious cults that declared the area to be the Promised Land, and in its inhabitants the remnant which God had preserved, like Noah and his family, as He rained down punishment on the rest of the globe for its transgressions.

Then the plague had come. The Acolytes said that the god had been there from the beginning, waiting while the most tenacious and resourceful men and women poured in from the surrounding territories. Once her domain had been thus enriched, she had breathed out her Sigh of Delight. Morgan remembered it, the strange smell in the air that evening, the tightening of the throat, and then the sounds of agony pouring in from all sides, the beating and clawing on the walls of the neighboring apartments, the cries for help as people collapsed in the streets, the frenzied wails of an infant and the screams of its mother as she begged for her child to be silent so that she could endure her agony in peace.

Morgan himself had crawled out onto the balcony, dark ribbons of pain tightening themselves around his heart, releasing, tightening, releasing, each time squeezing a little harder, the moments of relief only serving to freshen the pangs and keep blessed unconsciousness at bay.

In the morning, the dying had lain still. Not dead, but too exhausted from fighting against their illness to do more than occasionally twitch. Now and then the sound of a broken moan rose from the street to remind the living that others were still suffering too. Morgan had risen. He had felt frail and light, and for a moment he had imagined that he was a phantom, so tremulous and uncertain his body had seemed. The mirror had shown him pale, his face covered in sweaty grime, his eyes sunken and a shock of white hair hanging in a limp ringlet, framing one side of his face. The rest of his hair had remained black.

Water. Food. Several minutes listening to the buzz of the radio. He'd felt his strength returning and had collapsed on his sofa in a state of shock. Somehow when it had been happening somewhere else it had seemed like a horror movie: capable of turning your stomach, of making you start, of leaving you with a gnawing sense of terror that lingered into the night. But it hadn't seemed real.

"Help!"

The voice was coming from out in the hall, terribly weak.

"Please. Help."

Morgan had never really been the type to get involved. Heroism was for other people — people who knew what they were doing. Besides, he was sick himself and utterly exhausted.

"Please!" there was something about the anguish expressed in that plea. He had plied himself off the sofa and gone to the door.

The victim should have been a woman or a child, someone small and pitiable who he could have taken into his arms and nursed. It was a man, a neighbor from down the hall with short hair and the kind of sleeveless plaid shirt, beer-barrel stomach and tattooed arms that frightened Morgan. His eyes were glued half-shut and his body was covered in jeweled, ruby boils that stood out from his skin like bloodied crystals. Clutched in his arms was a whimpering dog that scratched and clawed, trying to escape from the vice of its owner's grip. Its nails burst one of the boils. The blood that spilled out was mixed with yellowish fluid and amber deposits of crystallized pus.

"Can I help you?" Morgan had asked stupidly.

The man had looked up, prying one of his eyes open. Morgan realized that it was only because of his tremendous strength that he had been able to crawl this far down the hall, that he was still able to speak. "My dog," the man had said, and released the animal into Morgan's arms.

By the fourth day all of the dying had been dead. Morgan had let the dog go: food had been scarce, the milk rations hadn't started yet, and in any case Morgan didn't like animals much. He'd spent the better part of a week trying to bury the other inhabitants of his apartment building, partly out of sentiment and partly because he didn't want some other infection, incubating in the decomposing flesh, to come wafting through his window at night. He'd buried twenty-six before succumbing to the magnitude of the task. Out of 145 tenants, he'd been the only one to survive. The remaining corpses he'd dragged out into the streets. A funeral pyre had been impossible, the risk of setting the surrounding buildings on fire too high. He'd had no choice but to leave them to rot.

A week later, on the first of May, the Acolytes had arrived. They'd taken down the names of the survivors, and informed them that all were now servants of the Nameless One. They'd demanded to know Morgan's profession, and since he didn't want to say "layabout and vagabond" he'd answered "artist." That was when the idol had been commissioned. He'd been signed up for the milk ration and given a year to complete the work.

The idol was shrouded in an old bed-sheet with a lilac-spray design. The Acolytes arrived in the evening and loaded it into the back of a truck. They controlled the gas pumps and were the only ones with vehicles, but it hardly mattered: there was nowhere to go. The next morning Morgan walked through the city to where the unveiling was supposed to take place.

He was not alone. Other survivors had apparently been summoned to the event and they slowly dribbled out of the buildings forming a rag-tag processions through the streets. By now the bodies had been cleared away by work-forces organized by the Acolytes. The trees were growing and flowers had stubbornly poked their heads up out of clouds of weeds.

As they reached the center of the square in front of the gallery, Morgan saw that a maypole had been erected. Figures clad in flowing gowns drifted around it, long streamers forming a web that bound a group of frightened men to the celebratory post. A monotonous voice was crying, "These are those who have resisted the Nameless One. These are those who serve her at the closing of her year." Morgan stopped and watched the faces, the brave attempts at stoicism. He wondered why they weren't singing and crying out slogans in defense of their ideals until one of them uttered a wordless cry and he saw that the man's tongue was swollen and bruised, studded with dozens of ruby rings that tore the delicate flesh.

The dance drew tighter. The masks of bravery began to fracture as the sharp-edged ribbons sliced across flesh. Morgan could see that two of the martyrs had managed to reach out to one another, their fingers twined together. This simple solidarity seemed to bring them comfort even as suffocating bands were wrapped across their noses and their mouths. As their bodies twitched and struggled a distant power station was goaded into action and for a moment a thousand windows brightened and traffic lights guided the non-existent cars through the empty streets. It lasted less than a minute before the hum of air-conditioners and the flashing neon promises in the shop windows went dead. It had been enough. The two friends whose fingers had sought each other out in martyrdom closed their eyes and Morgan almost imagined that beneath the ribbons he could see them smiling, remembering that somewhere out there humanity was still striving, unyielding against impossible odds.

Morgan hadn't been to the gallery since the Rising. The unveiling was supposed to take place within the central hall and there were some hand-painted signs indicating that a new show had been organized in honor of the Nameless One, that 17 of the city's most talented artists were paying homage to the god. The rest of the gallery had been stripped. It wasn't at all clear whether the works had been taken and enshrined in private homes, a reminder of the culture that had been, or whether they had been removed and destroyed.

The new gallery was filled with horrors illuminated by skylights and candles. Canvases roiled with nightmarish abstracts, and golden spiders perched atop piles of human skulls. Morgan's sculpture was in the back. He was guided towards it and told by an Acolyte to stand at attention and defend his work. There was no conversation to be had with the man: his eyes were sunk into impenetrable shadow and he had that look of someone drifting along on the breath of someone else's thoughts.

Straggling crowds had started to filter into the gallery. Usually you didn't ever see enough people in one place to give any suggestion of society, but the show must have drawn half the population of the city. Ghostly faces, tightly bound in the webs of their own suffering, haunted the room. Each of the artworks seemed to bring the viewers closer to despair. Morgan unveiled his idol and stepped back.

It was a long time before anyone came. Most viewers looked at a couple of the works and then stumbled to some recess along the wall, turning in on themselves as they curled into fetal balls.

After a while the Acolytes came and led them away. Morgan himself wanted to join them, but he'd been given orders and when necessary, one served.

At last a woman approached him. Morgan could see that she was pretty far gone, drifting, clouded eyes hardly seeming to take in the world that surrounded them. She stopped in front of the sculpture, looked into its eyes. Her expression was that of someone struck by an arrow and she fell to her knees in front of it. A moment later, another joined her, suffering the same strange fate. Morgan shifted uncomfortably, wondering what sort of monster he had wrought that it could fell those few who had survived the rest of the gallery.

Soon there were nearly a dozen worshipers kneeling before the thing. On the wall, there was a fire-ax in a glass casket, waiting for some calamity to justify its deployment. Morgan wondered if the Acolytes would stop him before he could get to it, break the glass, and destroy the terrible object, work of his hands. He took a tentative step. One of his audience, a woman, looked up. Her face was drawn and sallow but it had the look of a face that had once been full and plump. Milky tears were running down her cheeks, but her eyes were clear. She looked like a weeping child upon awakening.

"Are you the artist?" she whispered, looking around her to see if anyone was listening.

Morgan, cornered, replied, "I am."

A smile. It was a very long time since Morgan had seen one of those. Several others looked up furtively, barely daring to look at him. Their faces were covered in the same cloudy fluid. There were a few that Morgan had specifically identified as drifters, but now their eyes were clear and their grief was their own.

"Your bravery..." the woman shuddered. "Thank you."

An Acolyte was passing through the crowd towards them. Quickly, the woman lowered her head and resumed her silent prayers.

"What have you depicted?" the voice of the servant of the Nameless One sounded shaken.

"The plague, O Loyal One, in homage to the Mother of Plagues." Morgan could feel the nervousness in his own voice, the thin squeak like a broken clarinet.

The Acolyte stopped and looked at it. His eyes cast back and forth between the work and the artist. Morgan felt his chest tightening as it had during the plague.

"I tried to render faithfully --"

"I can see what you've tried to render."

Their eyes met and for a moment Morgan felt that he was being drawn deep into a well of darkness, the sort of place where a man would spend a long time drowning, with walls that would tear off his fingernails as he clawed them in despair. It was a long time since he'd felt real fear, and there was something almost enjoyable about it. A genuine emotion after months of drifting into hallowed numbness. "I meant no offense." He wasn't sure which frightened him more, the thought of the punishment the Nameless One inflicted on blasphemers, or the thought that they were going to destroy his work.

"Your work will be remembered." The Acolytes smile was terrible. "Do not forget this. Your work will be remembered. The Nameless One treasures the brave. They are the especial jewels in her crown." He withdrew a slip from his pocket, noted down Morgan's name from the hand-made plate at the statue's feet, handed it to him. It was a renewal of Morgan's milk allowance for the next year.

As the man continued on, Morgan looked around the gallery. Those who had not been able to brave more than the first few exhibits were being led away. The few who could stomach the work continued to drift towards his statue, to fall before it, to weep away the numbness that clouded their eyes. He recalled that the Nameless One had waited while her brethren had been feeding, had waited for the stalwart and resourceful to flock to her domain. He thought of the lights, every so often coming on in the darkness, and of how he had always wondered why sentries were not posted at the power plants, why this resistance was allowed to go on. He considered the ax again, and then considered the sort of bravery that would be required to wield it, the example he would set, the silent cheering of frightened hearts, the statement of a ruined idol in a hall full of monstrosities. Perhaps they would even drag him out, yelling oaths of rash defiance against the Nameless One, and they would offer the people the spectacle of martyrdom to stoke their hopes.

He shuddered. The milk-man had been right. Everything served the Nameless One and her designs. It was necessary. Everyone served.

Until the end of the day he remained, occasionally leaving his post to wander about the gallery, to look at the other works. Most of the artists were no longer present. They had joined their audiences, curled up against the wall. The few who remained were those works expressed something

18

different, a kernel of truth or beauty waiting in the darkness. Morgan didn't stop to talk to them, didn't meet their eyes. He wanted the savage emptiness of the display to overwhelm him so that he could join the huddled and the damned, so that he could be led away like the others, become numb, drift, and forget.

It was nearing the end of the day when finally he decided, he would go to the wall. He would crouch down. He would hold his head between his knees. He would force them to lead him away ignominious, anonymous, not brave, not a hero, not a jewel in her crown, simply a human being clutching his quiet dignity inside of himself where no one else would see it, where the Nameless One wouldn't know it, where it would be his alone.

He curled up, his stomach tightened with fear, bands of pain squeezing his heart, and he waited, listening to the quiet whimpers of those further down the wall. Eventually he rolled over, his arms wrapped around himself like a shell.

In the morning, the gallery had been still. All of the others had either left or been led away. Outside in the square there was a pile of fresh bodies, not yet dead, embracing and clawing at each other as the ruby boils erupted across their bodies. For a moment, the streetlights flickered and the sound of music could be heard for a couple of minutes playing from the loudspeakers in the square. From down the street, the tolling of the milk-man's bell rang out. A new year had begun.

Lubyanka

It was a cell-mate in the Lubyanka who told me that Stalin had once ordered a live chicken brought to him, for a demonstration. The great man plucked it, still alive. It flopped about in pain; it was covered in blood. Then he gave it a little handful of crumbs. He said that if you hurt an animal, then feed it, it will be loyal to you forever. This, he said, is true also of people. That was Moscow in my time: a city of plucked hens feeding from the hand of a tyrant.

When they came to arrest me, it was not on account of the mysterious deaths in the streets surrounding my apartment. You see, death was not such a mystery in those days. People were used to it. Swept it under the carpet, like the ashes of letters that they should have known better than to write. So it wasn't because of that.

The reason I was arrested was that there was a Party demonstration, and I was supposed to be there. I had made something of a minor hero of myself: making broken boilers continue to run when there was no money to repair them. They were dangerous, these boilers. In a year, perhaps less, one of them would explode, and most likely people would be killed. But for the moment, I was a hero; a man who made the impossible possible. I was supposed to give a speech. The only problem was, the speech was in the middle of the day, and I didn't have the fortune of bad weather to protect me from the sun.

I did have the fortune to be arrested at night: that is how they work, and it is very good for someone like me. The Black Maria pulled up quietly at the door below my apartment, and all of the nosy old ladies locked their doors and pressed their ears against the keyholes so they could try to figure out who had been arrested. There were seven, eight men. That many because I had not shown up to make a speech.

They told me to stand up against the wall, while they went through all of my things, looking for evidence. There was a book on engineering, written by a man who was a German and not a socialist. No doubt, I was in contact with this man. There was nothing else; even when they had pried up the mildewed floor-boards and torn apart the mattress where I had not slept in the months since I became what I am. The wooden box beneath the bed perplexed them: but they were so sure that it had been filled with illicit correspondence that they did not guess its purpose.

I could see the vein sticking out of the neck of the man who was holding the gun on me. His blood moved very fast. It is always that way with people who are not used to doing evil. The lips are set, and the eyes are very firm, and they've learned to obey, but the conscience -- yes, it is the conscience that drives the heart to such excesses. I would like to have drained him, but as I said, there were seven -- perhaps even eight -- of them, and I was only one. Anything less and I would not have hesitated.

In any case, it did not take very long. They did not like to make a big show: for themselves, once they were back at their lair and there was no one to see, yes. Then they like to show off. They like to parade around and pretend that they are Pharaoh. They are always sure that Moses will not prove able to part the Red Sea again. That is how it always is with men like that. But when they are out in the streets, and there are old ladies listening at keyholes, then they are swift. Then they move like urchin thieves through a crowd, pick-pocketing lives and always looking over their shoulders in case the right hand of God is moving up behind to cut them down. I half-intended to be the instrument of that wrath, but then, they were very efficient. With efficient men, it is difficult to know when to strike.

At first, when I was in the prisons, it was very good for me. You see, they put you in with a lot of men, and they are all strong men growing weaker, and they are all being made to turn pale and gray, and they don't let you get near a splinter of sunlight if they can help it. They deprive you of sleep, turning off and on the fly-specked lights night after night. But what need do I have of sleep? The light is electric: it hurts the eyes a little, but that is no great thing. They give you a lump of porridge, and if you lie back in your bunk and close your eyes at meal-time, pretending that you are asleep, you can be assured that some other man will snatch away your bowl and gobble down your portion. No one will see that you are not eating. There is no need to kill: no one is going to notice a little bite; a couple of little punctures on the arm. By the time that they are sleeping, they are dead to the world. The prison is crawling with tiny vampires: bedbugs, head lice. Another bite in the morning makes no difference. No one will be surprised to see them weakening so fast. Yes, it was very good for me at first.

The problem is that you are constantly being called in to be questioned. They pester you endlessly, walking up and down, shining lights at you, stripping off your clothes, waving about a gun and posturing like a louse who thinks he is Napoleon. This is of no consequence if you are not sleep deprived and hungry. What are they going to do? They can shout and tear down the walls until their necks begin to quiver like a shaken head-cheese. This is their problem. They are suffering more than me. It is almost amusing. Besides, if I give them a confession I could very well be doomed. I have learned, listening, that there are cracks in the roofs of the Stolypin cars that take you to the camps. Enough to let in the cold. Maybe enough to let the light in during the day. And once you get to gulag, you are always out-of-doors. Yes, it is best for me to remain here, being interrogated, where there is no risk of sunlight.

This is what I was thinking, until they decided that I ought to be confined alone. Separate a man, keep him from the company of fellows, put him in a cell as tiny as a coffin, do not let him sleep, bring him in every day, after eating a little spoonful of watery bread, and sit eating a fat pork roast in front of him. Surely that will break any man.

Perhaps. But is something like me a man? I have not decided this yet.

The problem is blood. The accommodation is comfortable enough. The bedbugs do not see with human eyes, and to their instinct, I am no more a man than is the stone wall. Cramped quarters are not an obstacle. But now they are keeping me alone. My hearing becomes more sensitive. I can hear the sound of the man in the next cell, beating on the wall, scratching at his skin. I do not know very well why people beat on walls. It is a mad instinct. Something irrational. But something that is from very deep in the psyche. I do not beat on my wall, but this is because I am less of a man. The man in the next cell is utterly human. I can hear his nails pulling up great swathes of scabby skin. I can hear the blood growing frenzied when he is about to start pumelling the concrete bricks. I can hear it slowing down when his heart becomes exhausted enough to endure captivity again. Then he resumes scratching, miserably, without hope of alleviating his sufferings. Yes. He will leave this place with an understanding of what it is to suffer. Either it will ruin him, and he will crawl out of that coffin, less a man than an insect, ready to give them all the satisfaction they desire -- these men who sate themselves on the ruin of the innocent. Either that, or it will prove a chrysalis, and will transform him into an angel. This is not a hope that I can entertain; I who share in his sufferings. And I do share them. Every time that his heart begins to rush, it is torture to me. A lash on my already overburdened hunger. Every time he scratches, I imagine that he has torn the skin, and the image of blood dripping from the scabs is like water poured out on the sand before a man dying of thirst. I envy the bedbugs that torment him. I am made even less human than I was when I began.

That is why, after four days of such confinement, when they bring me in to be examined about my deliberate insult to the Party, and to ask me about my connections to suspect groups of which I have never heard, and whose existence I doubt, I am not so prudent as I have been in the past. Here is this man. This little man. This Checkist. This rusted pipe through which suffering flows into the prison. This creature: he is covered in blood. It is on his hands. It fills his soul. It stains his conscience. The man in the cell next to me, the man who scratches and pounds the walls: he is a man. I would hesitate to kill him, even in my hunger. I would kill him. Yes. I don't deny what I have become. But I would hesitate for a moment, perhaps just for the sake of vanity, so that I could say that there was something human left in me. But this creature? No. This is a reservoir of blood, and I am hungry.

This is how they discover what I am. I am told to sit. There is a gun sitting on the table. It is pointed towards me. I am sure that it is not outfitted with silver bullets. They are asking me the same questions. I am looking at the hand on the gun. It is a fat hand, ugly, covered in blue veins. It is full of blood. I do not tolerate this for long. I grab the hand, because it is the closest thing. I sink my teeth into the wrist. They shoot me, of course, and that is painful. They club me across the back of the head with their toy rifles. Still, even then, they think that I am only an ordinary prisoner, driven mad by thirst, by anger, by sleeplessness -- who knows? They don't understand. Even the man whose life I am draining does not understand, though he feels that his heart is slowing too quickly, that this is not an ordinary wound. Death is not, however, a possibility that he has grappled with too deeply. He cannot bear to look it in the eye. His soul is too flabby to stand up and face it. This is not my concern.

In a place like this, there are a lot of men with guns. They arrive in the room, and they keep on shooting me until the pain is crippling. I would not have let go, even then, if there had been any blood left in him. But when the heart is so near to stopping, why suffer any more? I let him go, and hear him die a second later. I do not see it, because they throw a black cloth around my head, and kick me onto the ground, and shatter my chest with bullets until they cannot believe that I could possibly be alive. I think if I had not just eaten, it would have been very hard to recover. But the blood of the Checkist is not like the blood of the prisoners. It is not thin and anemic, but swollen and fat. I am very strong, and when they realize that I am still breathing, they are understandably afraid.

So what do they do? They call the man in charge, and he comes, and he sees the situation. By this time I am sitting in a chair again, and they have put me in handcuffs, and tied me around with chains, and then with chains again. Of what am I capable? This is what they are wondering. Will I break the chains like Sampson, and pull down the pillars of their puerile empire? I am not strong enough for that; but they do not need to know.

So the director, or whoever he is, comes in and looks at me. A medic with nervous hands pries open my mouth. The director sees the teeth. He sees the body of the interrogator, which they are wrapping up to take out. But what is he to do? Certainly there are old Romanian women in the building who could tell him everything that he needs to know. But he will not go and ask them. If he goes and he asks some babushka with a kerchief-ful of superstition how to deal with the vampyr, he will feel that he has sunk below his dignity. "When I am gone, she will blow her nose at me and laugh," he thinks. So he does not ask, and he does not learn. He would not even make a good vampire, this Sultan of the NKVD. You must begin with a soul if you are to have something to lose.

Perhaps there are tales that he has heard whispered in his childhood. But how can he be an important figure with a clove of garlic draped around his neck? How can he send a requisition for a box of silver bullets, when everybody knows that there is nothing in the world but machinery and bread. He cannot taunt me with a crucifix, and a bust of Lenin will hardly inspire my vampire blood to fear. If I was Hungarian, perhaps he could have tolerated it. Such inconsideration for the law of materialism might be forgiven in a Hungarian. But I am Russian. So he is impotent.

We sit that way for a long time, him and I. I was once known as a man who made possible the impossible. I was supposed to give a speech on how to do it. Every so often, he stands up and paces across the floor. He is thinking of making a telephone call. Of asking for back-up. He is thinking about whether he will have to arrest the men who have seen what has happened. Perhaps he noticed some of them making the sign of the cross. Perhaps he is merely afraid.

It is this image of him: the puny Napoleon ruminating on his Waterloo, that brings me comfort now. He did not beat me. He has confined me, yes. Sent me to a concrete closet deep within the heart of the Lubyanka. Sentenced me to hunger. To eat bedbugs for the little drop of human blood that they have stolen. It is no sort of life. But when this empire of the puny has dissolved, and this tomb has become an abandoned admonition, he will be gone, and I will be here.

SCHRÖDINGER'S ZOMBIE

"Do you think that they're intelligent?" Whispered, in the darkness.

"Zombies are practically by definition unintelligent. They're human beings minus intelligence. People reduced to their appetites and passions."

"No. Not passions. They're entirely devoid of passion. That's part of why we're so afraid of them. That and the fact that they want to eat our brains."

The younger one shakes his head. "This isn't Plants vs. Zombies. The whole 'brains' thing is just a cheesy stereotype. They're cannibals but they'll probably take your arm just as happily as your frontal lobe."

The boys are huddled near a gabled window. One is an artist, slender, dark-haired, dressed in a lovely pea-green coat. The other is a Stoic, wearing an old cardigan, a Roman haircut and a worn t-shirt.

It's dark and they can't make out anything down below, but the fine spray of pin-prick starlight is somehow comforting. Besides, the window gives the impression that they are gathering intelligence, that if something happened down there they might see.

"You're deflecting attention away from my central point," the artist whispers. "They're not just "human beings minus intelligence." They are also human beings divorced from the capacity to love, to feel, to indulge in empathy, to appreciate the image of eternity in a wildflower. They are utterly indifferent to the works of van Gogh."

From the far side of the attic there is the sound of a trap door very quietly closing. The two fall silent, hardly breathing. A hunched figure picks its way across the cramped space. The artist readies his lighter next to a pile of kindling scavenged from around the attic. In the event that it becomes necessary, the house is old and dry. It'll go up fast.

"Who says they're indifferent to Starry Night? Whenever I see a throng a zombies standing around in the street they're always just looking straight ahead, staring, not really doing or saying much of anything. Maybe they're sunk deep in aesthetic contemplation." The voice is human, their brother's. He reaches into the pocket of his black leather jacket and take out a pack of cigarettes.

The artist lowers his lighter and replies somewhat waspishly, "They are not. You can tell by the soulless expression on their faces. They're not contemplating anything, just standing about waiting for prey."

The smoker lights his cigarette in a corner, far from the window. "Have you ever watched yourself draw? Half the time you're looking off into space with an expression like a hollow turnip. Obviously if someone is contemplating the beauty of a landscape or the curve of a youthful thigh you can see that they're engaging with their environment. But if they're contemplating how the youth's thigh is actually an expression of the beauty of the Laws of Athens and the cosmic splendor of the first cause, then they kind of look spaced out. Maybe zombies are really the next stage in the evolution of humanity. Maybe they are actually more, and not less intelligent than us."

The Stoic looks pained. "That's stupid. First of all, zombies are wholly irrational."

"Prove it."

"I don't have to 'prove it.' It's obvious. You can't reason with a zombie. You'd be crazy to try."

"Sure, but you're collapsing rationality to the function of dialectic reasoning through the medium of human language which is clearly a limited and reductionist definition. I mean, when a severely autistic kid is sitting there staring out into space and contemplating the mathematical relationships in a spider web the kid is certainly engaging in intelligent rational analysis even though he exhibits a total incapacity for dialectic philosophy."

"Right...but now you're drifting into Popper's dolls territory. You're suggesting that maybe zombies are rational even though they display absolutely no observable rational characteristics. Your argument is that their rationality cannot be engaged by another reason, which means that your thesis is unfalsifiable."

"Holy epistemological chauvinism Batman! Since when is your capacity to observe a phenomenon the sine qua non of its ontology? That's like saying that because a mouse can't read Plato, Plato isn't intelligible. Obviously we can't engage with them rationally, but that doesn't mean they're not engaging rationally with one another. I mean, look at how many of them there are. Usually this place would get like four visitors in a month, but there are dozens of them down there. They must be communicating somehow."

"You can't deduce anything from the congregation of zombies around their prey. It's like proposing that flies are telepathic because they congregate around roadkill."

"Flies can smell meat from 7 kilometers away. There's no evidence that zombies can smell us, and it's just as likely that their condition grants them some form of telepathy as that it grants them enhanced olfactory super-powers. We don't know what they're capable of, only that they're capable of something that we're not. Which means it's perfectly possible that they are communicating."

"Even if they are, we can clearly observe that they are not engaging in rational or moral deliberation. Like that woman back at the diner. She attacked her own children without even thinking about it. No pause. No hesitation. She didn't stop to consider whether it was a good course of action or not, she just did it."

"How do you know she didn't deliberate?"

"Because she acted immediately without stopping to consider what she was doing, and displayed no expression of internal conflict whatsoever."

"So moral deliberation exists only where there is evidence of a conflict between competing passions? Stop me if I'm wrong, but I would have assumed that for a Stoic the ideal form of moral deliberation would be dispassionate. That a soul in a state of perfect equilibrium would be able to quickly and decisively survey its moral options and move towards action without first having to engage in the kind of agonistic indecision that evidences itself through visible grimaces and white-knuckles."

"Right. But there's a huge difference between immediately and dispassionately moving towards the good, and immediately and dispassionately doing evil. One is an expression of rationality, the other is bestial."

The smoker shrugs and takes a drag, "I think you're taking a wholly vivicentric view of the situation. You're assuming that being eaten and becoming a zombie is bad. But what would Epictetus say? It's external. It's beyond your control. You may think it's bad, but that's only your opinion. "

"The loss of my rational freedom and moral capacity would definitely be bad! That is rationally provable. All other misfortunes that could befall a man are only perceived to be evil, and can be appreciated as being in accord with nature. The loss of myself is the one thing that is truly intrinsically evil, and that cannot be construed to be otherwise."

"But your proof that zombies are irrational and amoral rests on the assumption that one must take as a first principle that 'being alive is preferable to being undead.' Look at that zombie mother: maybe she was in a state of zombie ecstasy. Maybe the scales had fallen from her eyes, and she had just emerged from Plato's cave and was stunned by the dazzling beauty of undeath. Maybe she was eager that her children should join her on the zombie plateau. From her point of view, she might have been saving them from the agonies and anxieties of earthly life and translating them into a state of perfect equilibrium and indifference. Maybe she knew that they would experience pain and suffering when her teeth ripped into their tender flesh, but she also knew that the suffering would be brief and the rewards great."

"That's bullshit." The artist toys with the lid of his lighter but doesn't dare light it. He's sure that the horde is still gathered there in the yard, but so far they haven't assailed the house. It's not clear whether they're waiting for something, or whether they're confused. Either way, one flicker of firelight could be enough to goad them into action. "The whole reason that the undead are terrifying is that they are a perversion of immortality. They represent the perpetuation of corporeal existence in the absence of spiritual life. They are an image of Hell. They're not on some sort of noble Manichean crusade to divest the living of their bodily burdens."

"Prove it."

"No. You're just being a dick. You don't want to become one of them any more than we do."

"Maybe not, but I'm open to the possibility that my fears are irrational. I'm not just playing devil's advocate here. I'm trying to think this through. 'Cause we know that if you burn them, they actually die, and we know that if you burn this house down we are going to actually die. So it's not entirely an academic point."

This gives the artist pause. But not for long. "I think I'll take my chances with the almighty, rather than with the undead."

"We're not getting into the God argument again. I'll be surprised if we're still here in the morning, and I doubt we're going to get that one cleared up by then. I think it would be more fruitful to at least consider the possibility that being undead is not conterminous with being brain-dead. Think about Omega Man for example. When the zombies are allowed to have dialogue, we're able to see their thought processes — and their thought processes are not entirely unrelatable."

"You're moving the goalpost," the Stoic interrupts. "The 'zombies' in Omega Man are clearly still in possession of some rationality. They are capable of language, and organization, they have an ideology and they are not undead. But here we're talking about Romero style zombies. Cannibalistic corpses, not people with a weird disease."

The artist shakes his head. "How on earth do you know that?"

"Well, I don't exactly. But since you forgot to charge your phone, we don't have internet access and I can't exactly Google it. I'm just going by what I've seen, and based on what I've seen this looks less like 28 Days Later and more like Dawn of the Dead."

"Forgive me if I'm showing my ignorance of obscure horror trivia, but wouldn't it be true that if a zombie is categorically different from a diseased human being — that is, if it's a difference of kind and not merely of condition — then strictly speaking it wouldn't be cannibalism. Not that I want to support him," he jabs his thumb out in the direction of the smoker. "But it does seem that if they are actually 'undead' that would involve a kind of indelible transformation. They would become a different species. Like, for example, that woman attacking her own children. It's obviously horrific from the children's point of view, but it's only a moral atrocity if we suppose a continuation of personality. I mean, when a newborn baby turns and suckles at the breast it doesn't stop to consider the moral implications of this action. It doesn't contemplate whether it is hurting its mother. It probably isn't conscious that the breast has any direct connection to the womb that it just vacated. It is hungry, and it eats. All of the zombies that we've seen are basically newborns. They haven't really had time to develop their faculties, to navigate their existential position within the universe, to develop a sense of identity."

"So you're positing that a capacity for morality and rationality exists in those things, and that over time they will come to manifest more overtly human behaviors?"

"Why more overtly human behaviors?" the smoker's cigarette has gone out. Damned cheap manufacturing. "Does not the excellence of a horse consist in it behaving excellently as a horse? Does not the excellence of a man consist in his behaving fully as a man? Does not it then follow, slave, that the excellence of a zombie consists in its behaving not like a man, but like a zombie?"

"Yes. But the question is whether zombies, as a species, possess intelligence, rationality, and moral capacities that would render them deserving of the same kind of consideration that we extend to human beings. If a zombie is basically just the host for a parasite that consumes human flesh and perpetuates itself by manipulating the nervous systems of its victims, yes, consuming human flesh and infecting people would be excellent after the kind of that particular parasite — but when we encounter a cancer or a virus that behaves excellently as a cancer or a virus we do not then conclude that it ought to be celebrated and valorized by human beings. Your original hypothesis was that zombies are an evolution of humanity, not just a degradation."

"Right, but as a more evolved species we should not judge the success of the zombie individual in terms of whether it would be excellent if it were human. That was my point."

"But my point is that if zombies are in fact superior to man in a hierarchy of beings, then they would have to display superior characteristics."

He gets his cigarette relit. It tastes like ash. "Sure. Zombies are more efficient than human beings. They have more leisure. Their appetites are simple and unitary, leaving them free for unrestrained contemplation whenever they are not feasting on human flesh. They are indifferent and uneffected by their passions. They live in a society of perfect harmony. Zombies will attack other species, but they never engage in intra-species conflict. They are not troubled by externals. They have no worldly ambitions. They are unconcerned with culinary, sartorial or sexual pleasures. In fact, zombies are pretty much completely without vice. Even when they attack people there's no malice in it. The zombie exists in a state of perfect interior freedom, it fulfills its needs simply without guilt, pride, shame or anger. Although a zombie may be subject to the corruption of its flesh, it experiences neither pain nor mortality. On the whole, I think that to a Stoic that should serve as a pretty exhaustive demonstration of the superiority of zombie kind."

The artist presses his face towards the window. A sliver of moon has come out from behind the trees, and he's pretty sure that he can see movement. "I think its a pretty exhaustive demonstration of the inadequacy of stoicism."

"Shhh."

The Stoic looks unimpressed. "Yeah, yeah. I got the joke. But the entire argument is premised on the assumption that there is something going on inside the zombie's head. That we're seeing the decayed external vessel of an elevated internal self. I don't see any evidence to substantiate that claim. What I see is a rotten corpse that wants to rip me open and feast on my intestines. I see a being whose behavior is entirely driven by a monomaniacal appetite, a creature that is non-functional except when it is able to feed. I admit that there is a very small chance that its external behavior is deceptive, that it is actually engaged in lofty contemplation, and that its body has become an almost extraneous complication that it largely ignored. I also admit that it's possible that zombies possess the capacity for rationality and that given time they will go on to develop language and culture. If those things are the case, then it is only my human opinion that it is bad to be a zombie. But I don't think it's likely."

There's a sound downstairs, something twisting the doorknob. The smoker is barely stopping now to breathe in between puffs. He lights another cigarette off of the first one. For a moment the attic is illuminated. They've built up a very large pile of kindling, and a couple of gas cans are standing by ready to fuel the flames. There's a sound of cracking wood below, and the scraping of a bookcase that had been barring the front door. "I don't know if it's likely or not, but the question is quickly ceasing to be academic."

Rite of Atonement

The iridescent inks sparkled beneath her skin, each tattooed scale containing the secret symbols by which the waiting throng had chosen to express their darkest sins. The glittering ink would have proved poisonous over the years, infecting her mind with metallic madness, but this did not matter. Stretching before her were not years, but minutes. The beauty of the work was justified by its end.

She was his masterpiece, ten years in the making, chosen in childhood and transformed. He had performed over a thousand surgeries on her to make her what she was. Her jaw alone had been sawed and extended twenty-seven times before he had managed to warp the bone settings and stretch the skin enough to hold the juvenile crocodile bones that he had prepared to replace her human features. Now it projected six glorious inches from her natural jaw, and the sharpened teeth rose like ranks of ivory from the delicate flesh of reconstructed gums.

The new jawbone had inverted her nostrils, and in the reconstruction of her nasal passages he had made a series of precisely curved, parallel scars that tapered out beneath the sockets of her eyes. These had been dyed a deep green, with touches of yellow to accentuate the reptilian cast that it leant it to her face. The eye sockets themselves had been enlarged slowly, carefully scraping back the bone until the dyed-red irises peered out from deep caverns in her skull. Her hair had been blighted to its root, and in its place a line of poached rhinocerous horns, bolted into her skull, tapered down from her forehead to the base of her neck.

Wherever skin had proved unwilling to stretch any further, he had aided it with grafts taken from her tightly contracted waist. Inside, her stomach had been cut back and stapled to make her thinner, but it had been long time since she had been able to eat ordinary food, and the thick sludge that her feeding tubes pumped into her was already digested enough that the stomach was almost an unncessary complication. Her breasts had been cut away and the skin stretched taut across beautifully defined ribs, inked in shining yellow-white to look like the segmented stomach of a serpant. The muscles of her thighs had been electrically stimulated until they were as thick and strong as a well-trained runner's, but they rested on cleft feet, where ranks of metatarsals had been reorganized into three splayed toes. Her arms had been shortened: humerus, radius and ulna cut back, and her fingers artificially inflicted with osteo-arthritis until they bent and crooked into the claws of a hag, each finger ending in a long and sharpened talon.

But these were not his great achievements. Any Scapegoat, made by any Bone-Sculptor might have been subjected to the same metamorphoses. The high expression of his art was to be found on her back. There, attached to the base of her spine, was a crocodile's tail, the nerves carefully grafted into her spinal column, her mind trained over years to accept and control the alien appendage. This too, though, he had done before, even if he was the only Sculptor in the world who could have achieved such perfect dehumanization. What he had never before produced with such success, were the wings. No living animal possessed wings of such breadth, no systems for controlling them existed to be pillaged. He could not simply lay out a sacrifical vulture, and under the appropriate signs, in the proper time of the moon, delicately excise its quiverring neurons. The bones, the muscles, the sinews, the nerves, all had to be custom crafted; ivory replicas of the fossilized bones of ancient dragons clothed in artificial tissues and vat-grown veins. It had taken a year for her brain to realize that they were there, years more for it to learn to flex the muscles, until now, at last, she was capable of stretching out those shining wings and holding them taut as a bird in flight.

She would not be able to fly, of course, but he had run the simulations carefully, had seized his achievement in the animated projections of the contact-lens computer screen that nestled against his natural eye. She would be chased to the cliff's edge just like all the others, but when she arrived she would not tumble graceless to the stones. She would spread wide those gossamer-green contructs of his genius and for a few precious moments that wind would fill them and she would glide until the weight of her body broke the fragile bones of the living apparatus that held her aloft. Then she would fall like a wounded bird, like Icarus as he plunged, spinning, downwards from the sun. In a tangle of broken wings, she would carry all of the terrors and tortures that he had perpetrated against her down to be drowned in the depths of the sea.

She was ready. Her body shone green and azure in the first glimmers of the sunlight that inched through the opened door of the wooden cart in which, by tradition, she had been carried to this place. A path of beaten black gravel stretched out from the door, leading down to the point on the cliff from which, each year, the sacrifice was flung. All who had paid for her making stood along the roadway, clad in long robes, their faces concealed behind the grotesque masks that they would burn once darkness fell. The record of their evils was recorded on her body. Today, with her, that record would be washed away. They turned towards her, simple weapons readied in their hands, prepared to chase the monster from their midst.

She stumbled out. Her gait was awkward, stilted. It was a long time since she had been capable of human speech, but her throat produced a thin keening of alarm. She turned her ponderous deformities around, trying to clamber back into the safety of the cart, but the horses were quicker — before she could complete a turn, the cart was gone. The crowd closed in, leering over her, leaving the gravel path and the point of the cliff as the only way in which to escape. Her maker leaned towards her ear and whispered, "Run, run towards the water. You can escape them, and all their cruelty. I have given you the power to fly!"

Not for several years had the tortured muscles of her face been capable of expression, but something flickered now, in the deep chasms of her eyes. He saw that she knew he was lying. Some incomprehensible admonition gurgled in the depths of her stretching throat, and then she turned towards the cliff. Those whose sins she carried in her skin pressed forward, goading her with whips, pelting her with stones, screaming and prodding her towards the cliff's edge.

The sunlight flashed into her eyes as she looked out over them, as she looked up towards the distant sky. Then, like a seraph before the throne of God, she folded her beautiful wings across her face, knelt down on the road and would not be moved. No torment or deprecation would raise her to her feet, or bring her one step closer to the cliff. At last, in a frenzy of wrath, the masked figures fell on her. Their clubs and the rocks shattered her fragile jaw, tore the delicate fabric of her wings, crushed the carefully crafted bones, until at last her shoulders ceased shivering at the blows and they saw that she had died. They stopped, then, horrified to see their sins written out across her back, the blood of their transgressions crying out from stones.

Birth of a Kingdom

My secret was discovered in a singularly unpleasant way. In the explosion, my left hip had been badly burnt. Slick sacks of skin had sloughed away from my midriff and the threads of my uniform had become fused with the sizzling flesh. At the field hospital, they tore the pants free without ceremony or anesthetic. Amidst my screams I heard the gasping confusion of the orderlies, the quick dismissals. The disapproving face of a doctor loomed over me. He said nothing, but turned my face from side to side, evaluating the look of hard determination in my eyes. I had stopped screaming, set my face like a stony death-mask. It wasn't easy, but I would not have him accusing me of weakness.

"Private... I'm sorry, this says that your name is Charles. I assume that is not the case."

Charles was my older brother, a boy of delicate features with a poetic disposition.

"Marjorie," I admitted. "My name is Marjorie." I closed my eyes and breathed into the pain. "I've fought bravely," I said, "as bravely as anyone. I've been wounded for my country." I opened my eyes and gazed at him as clearly as I could. "I deserve to have my secret kept."

He raised one eyebrow. "I was not the only one present, young lady, when you were undressed."

The burning sensation was building again, a bubble of lava pressing against the hardened surface of my will. I craned my neck back, fists tightening, trying to hold myself in check. I heard the doctor calling for morphine, felt a blanket placed over me to protect my modesty. There was a soft prick, and then a rushing sensation of relief as the pain subsided to bubble quietly deep beneath the skin. As I faded into sleep I heard the doctor promise, "I'll do what I can."

Charles would not have survived the war. I'd seen it in his eyes the day that he'd opened the letter which summoned him to the front. His fingers shaking, he'd handed it across the table to our mother who had placed it down before us with tears in her eyes.

"I have been called to die," he said simply, staring glassily into a plate of steamed beans.

Later, as he paced his room that night, I had heard him muttering to himself. They were strange incantations, alien words that I had heard several times before as I lay in my bed on the other side of the wall. I had always imagined them to be the voice of Nightmare speaking to me from the edges of sleep. Now, as I stood outside of his room I realized that this bizarre, croaking, almost blasphemous voice was no echo from the Outer Darkness, but rather the voice of my own brother speaking to the night.

I pushed open the door. He turned to me, startled, and slammed shut the top of his secretary desk. A small brass key remained in the lock, unturned. There was a strange smell, not exactly unpleasant. Dark and smokey, like chocolate burnt in an Aztec brazier. "Marjorie," he said in alarm. "I thought you were in bed."

"I couldn't sleep," I settled myself in his bed, pulling the covers up over my knees. My night-dress was too short, really, but I couldn't justify the expense of material for another. Not when everything was needed for the war effort. "I was thinking about what you'd said."

He turned to his desk and began to shuffle his books. I could see that he was trying to make it look like a nervous tick, but in fact he was secreting a small, dark volume in between a Bible and the plays of George Bernard Shaw. "About my death?" he said. There was something nasty in his tone.

"Why are you so sure that you'll die?"

He turned his eyes warily towards me. I realized that he had been carrying a burden of fear in his heart ever since the papers had announced that there would be conscription. "I've seen it," he said. "I've been seeing it since I was a child. Clouds of dust and smoke. My body thrown into the air. A fire burning away my skin. And then the heaven splitting open the shell of an egg." He shuddered and settled himself on the edge of his desk, shaking his head morosely. "The shell of an egg spilling me out, naked, into a world... I can't describe it. I wouldn't dare."

Gloomy visions were about the last thing in the world to worry me. "Charles, honestly," I said. "It's okay that you're afraid to go to war. Just because you're a man... it doesn't guarantee that you'll have the stomach for such things." He looked at me coldly, but I continued anyway, "Any more than being a woman guarantees that I won't." I waited until the hostility in his eyes had slightly dimmed and then began to outline my plan.

He turned away from me, looking out the window into the starless night. After a long time he said, "Maybe. Maybe even prophecy can be averted. Perhaps my prayers have been heard."

The essence of the plan was simple. I would arrange to spend the summer with some relations on the east coast, and he would go away to war. Only in fact, he would go to the coast and continue with his poetry and his anthropological researches, as he called them. I would cut my hair, bind my breasts, and board ship for Europe. He would put it out that he had been turned away from military service for medical reasons so that there would be no question of dirty looks or white feathers. I would write him letters from the front, and he would translate them into his own hand and his own idiom before sending them along to mother at home. I would also enclose letters from myself, giving rambling, content-free accounts of intrigues with various local boys and the state of the petunias in Cousin Helena's garden. In this way we would maintain the illusion that I was enjoying a vacation by the sea, and that he was fighting in the trenches. By fall, the war would almost certainly be over and I would return home. Complications, like going to the bathroom or taking showers without my femininity being observed, I figured I would work out along the way.

As the date for our departure drew near, his nervousness increased. I thought that he was frightened of being found out and jailed for having tried to evade service. Sleeplessness began to haunt his eyes, and every time that I came into his presence he would suddenly look guilty. The night before our train left I heard him pacing up and down in his room. I was also unable sleep. For several weeks I had been reading recruitment posters and listening to the stories of men who had come back from the front to stir up the courage of those who had yet to enlist. The war seemed like a glorious adventure in an exotic land, rich with history. I might see Napolean's arch in Paris, or march past the Colisseum in Rome. Even if I was stationed somewhere dull, like Belgium, I would still get to cross the Atlantic and prove myself, living as a man among men. I was certain, in any case, to avoid the tedium of knitting socks, fermenting sauerkraut, and waiting anxiously to hear news of the menfolk.

It must have been nearing the first light of dawn when I heard an odd clatter from Charles' room. It sounded like a window opening, and someone trying to squeeze through. Creeping out of my bed, I ventured into the hall and made my way along in the moonlight. A candle was still blazing in my brother's room. I tried to peer in underneath the door but I couldn't make out anything except a fluid pool of candle-light shifting in the breeze. "Charles?" I knocked gently, whispering. There was no response. The door was locked, but the locks were simple and easily forced. It was a trick that I had learned a long time ago, as a girl, and it had allowed me to gain access to all kinds of forbidden knowledge and hidden sweets.

The room was abandoned, the window opened on the cold spring night. There was the same strange scent as before, only it was much stronger now. A small brass crucible in the centre of the room contained the remains of some sort of resinous insense. The fumes were powerful, and as I bent my head over the crucible there was a moment of intense dizziness. I felt deeply uneasy. Charles spoke rarely about his research, always saying that it was too technical to be of interest. Once my mother had extracted a page of notes from one of his diaries, but it had been exceedingly dull reading, detailing the descendents of a particular individual who had immigrated to New England in the 1740s. We had returned it quietly and agreed to give my brother his privacy. After all, he did occasionally send and receive correspondence from a Professor at Miskatonic University and the thought that her son might one day pursue higher learning excited my mother tremendously.

Now, as I shivered in the darkness, marking the full, pale moon that hung in a sickly sheathe above the dark horizon, I no longer felt that privacy was in order. I tried to open the cupboard at the top of his desk, but the key had been removed and I quickly discovered that my skills were not equal to the delicate little lock. I could have broken it, but it was an expensive piece of furniture and one of the few nice things in the house leftover from before Father had passed away. I contented myself instead with searching for the small black book that he had concealed.

At first, it seemed to be nowhere in the room but then I accidentally knocked the Bible from his bedside table. It fell open on the ground, revealing that the words of Holy Scripture had been hollowed out and this little volume put in their place. The edges of the hollow had been blackened with fire. A little of the text remained in the margins and several passages looked as though they had been overwritten in a kind of dark rust-brown ink. I removed the black book and quickly searched his bookshelf for another of similar dimensions. A small Latin dictionary with a dark blue cover seemed a good substitute. I placed it inside of the gutted Bible and then snuck out of the room, taking the little black volume with me. Although I intended to read it that very night, and to return it in the morning, the scent of the strange incense had left me feeling slightly ill. I lay down, just until the nausea passed. I fell asleep.

When I woke in the morning, the remnants of a very strange dream were clinging to my consciousness. They were quickly whisked away by the forced-smiling, nervous activity of my mother as she prepared us for our journey and prepared herself to wave her son goodbye. I packed the black book in my handbag. We had a long train ride ahead of us, and it was a small book. I would read it while Charles was sleeping, and return it to his things when we reached our cousin's house.

I feel asleep in the arms of morphia. The hall to which the drug carried me was familiar. I had caught glimpses of it before, in the long nights in the trenches. Arcades of improbable height and impossible angles rose up overhead, finally meeting in a series of domes built around an alien geometry. The stars were painted on the roof, but there was something amiss about them. Every time that my eye tried to fix on a particular constellation there was a sense of vertigo, as though the stars were like eyes being pried from the heavens by my gaze. As the face of heaven was stretched and contorted, all of the other stars stared down at me with increasingly ominous accusation until, at last, I cast my eyes down. I could still feel the weight of opprobation hanging over me, but I didn't sense that I was committing any further transgression.

Keeping my eyes on the floor, I slowly made way down the hallway. There were side passages that broke off here and there, long galleries that stretched away to the right and to the left. Their floors seemed to dip and curve, and there were staircases the bent away from the hall like broken limbs. Something about their form was eerily familiar. As I walked passed, I stared down the passages, trying to place their sinister architecture.

At length I came to a central rotunda. In the middle there was a fountain that seemed to throw up plumes of bright orange-green flame that turned to liquid in the air and then descended, hitting the basin in a puff of ash. A soggy grey cloud spread out from it and as I approached I felt my lungs seizing up. I backed away, thinking perhaps that I should go back and try one of the side corridors.

When I turned around, however, I could see that I was being tailed by two creatures. They had the shape of men, but when they breathed out I could see a ghastly yellow vapour trailing up into the air. They wore strange uniforms, with high helmets and visors that covered their faces. Something about this armour suggested the translucent amber carapace of a junebug. They stood at a fair distance from me, and so long as I stood still they were also still. When I started to move towards them, however, they moved towards the centre of the hallway and I could feel in their eyes the same killing intensity that had been in my own eyes when I had stared across no-man's land towards the distant enemy lines.

Going back was obviously not an option. I circled around the fountain, clinging to the walls, covering my face with my sleeve in an attempt to keep the noxious mist at bay. As it condensed on my skin, I could feel it burning, leaving an oily grey-green stain. My breathing was strained and painful, and when I began to run I felt as though there was a stinging acid flowing through every capillary of my body. Fortunately, it did not last long. As soon as I had circumnavigated the fountain I found myself at the bottom of a steep staircase and I quickly climbed up out of the heavy cloud. The air was not fresh here — it smelled strange and metallic — but at least it didn't burn. I sat on the steps for a couple of minutes and refreshed myself, trying to wipe the last of the stinging droplets from my hands and my face.

When I was ready to stand up, I looked down at the fountain. The two creatures who were following me were standing there, barely visible through the cloud. They were perfectly still, keeping the precise distance that they had kept back in the hall. If they felt any discomfort, there was nothing to suggest it. I looked up the staircase. It was a long ascent, and reminded me of a picture that my brother had once shared with me, a picture from an archeology book of a steep stair rising to the top of a pyramid in a jungle. At the top there had been a sacrificial altar, and Charles had explained to me that once, in the distant past, human beings had been offered there to gods whose names no living tongue could pronounce. The stair was similar, even though there was no pyramid or jungle to pronounce it. A sense of dread seized me, but I could not bring myself to descend back into that burning cloud.

I began to climb.

The book did not get read on the train. It turned out that the nervous excitement, which had robbed me of so much sleep the night before, gave way to a kind of gloomy anticipation. I was restless, and wanted the journey to be over. Charles was particularly disagreeable and behaved as though somehow by allowing me to take his place he was doing me a favour. When I pointed out that I was doing this for him, he glared at me as though I had just mortally insulted him and said, "You're the one who doesn't want to see me dead."

I sank back petulantly into my seat, leaned my head against the window and stared out at the scenery until the train had rocked me to sleep.

By the time I awakened, we were at our destination. Cousin Helena was there with her husband and her new baby to pick Charles up. I went and helped him to settle in, but I was worrying about a thousand details: I needed to get my hair cut, to make sure that my papers were in order, to polish my boots. In less than twenty-four hours I was going to be a military man, and I had never been a man before nor had I ever been a soldier. Charles' book was forgotten entirely until the last minute. I shoved it into my knapsack and forgot about it again.

It wasn't until I was in France, sitting in a trench, watching the shells bursting overhead, that I recalled the book at all. I took it out of my pack. In the dim light I could see that there was a kind of oily film on the surface of the parchment cover. I opened it.

There were no words. The pages at first seemed blank, but as I looked at them an increasing sense of uneasy tension began to spread through my body. I felt at first as I had felt the first time that one of my comrades had brought out a pornographic book and showed around the pictures: a kind of slimy feeling that seemed to separate me from my own skin, and with it a sense of inexplicable shame. As I looked through Charles' book, however, this simple reaction developed into a deep revulsion and then fear. I felt as though I were staring into a featureless white abyss. Worse, I felt as though it were staring back at me.

I shut the book and put it back in my backpack. It was only when I tried to tie shut the small pocket that I realized that my hands were shaking. This was not good. Clearly, the book contained nothing. It was just a notebook. It seemed it had never even been used. My nerves were the problem. A shell whined overhead and exploded. Several small pebbles rained down on my helmet. I had been out here less than a month, and my nerves were starting to go. If I suffered a break-down, I would be hospitalized. If I were hospitalized I would be examined. If examined, my sex would be revealed.

I lit a cigarette. I needed to steady myself. I needed to be brave.

I climbed. The top of the stair did not end in a hideous pagan temple. There was no dark-skinned priest with a wicked obsidian knife. Rather, there was a pool like in an ancient bath. Steam rose from the surface, and floating on it were bodies. The bodies were silent, staring up into space. They had no clothing, and so it was possible to see that most were badly injured. Some were missing limbs, others had burns over most of their bodies. There was one whose stomach wall had been turned inside out, and I could see that bile was slowly leaking out into his intestines.

When I looked at them, I felt nothing. These injures were, in my opinion, all survivable. These men would crawl out of this pool and go on to live, taking their broken bodies and their memories with them back to their homes and their families. I had seen much worse. Indeed, there was something almost comforting about the presence of such familiar forms of suffering in the midst of so much that was impossible to explain.

I stepped towards the edge of the pool. It was now, as I reached the poolside, that I was able to see into the water. The pool had no floor, or at least none that could be seen. Long fronds, like rooted eels or serpentine seaweed rose up from an unfathomable bottom. I could now see that many of these were burrowing into the bodies of the injured. A faint, slow sucking motion shivered through their dark, opalescent skin. The men stared at the ceiling where the same twisted contellations looked down, sparkling with obscene delight.

There was no way around the pool. This was all there was.

Behind me, coming up the stairs, were the two figures that had been following me from the beginning. They were no longer hanging back. I could now see that their eyes were the same as the stars in the ceiling but that they had human faces. As they opened their mouths, I saw that insides were pools like the pool in front of me now. It took me a moment to realize that their uniforms were still wet, as though they had just dragged themselves out of the water. Slowly, converging towards me as they approached, they made their ascent.

The dreams had been easy to explain. Nightmares, from which I would awaken shrieking. My close comrades twitted me about it, telling me that in the night I screamed like a girl. Perhaps some of them suspected. I don't know. If they did, nothing was said.

It was the war, of course. The horrors which my feminine mind was unprepared for. Nothing in the recruitment pamphlets had suggested this. Nothing in the stories that men had told returning from the front. The adventure was a nightmare. So it hardly surprised me when its horrors claimed my dreams.

"Dream the world into being. Dream the world into waking. Bathe in the dreamworld. Drown in the dream."

These words, slowly, quietly whispered up from the mouths of the men sleeping in the water. Looking into the distance, I could see that there was a landscape growing, a landscape formed out of the malformed horrors that they had brought with them to this place. Columns that seemed to be made of shrapnel flying into a fiery sky, caught and molded in glass and metal. Hallways that twisted like coils of barbed wire. Explosions that created new constellations and blackened the day-time sky.

The men with the star eyes, and the insect armour walked towards me, backing me towards the edge of the pool. I planted my feet and held my ground, watching their approach. As soon as the first had reached the top of the stairs, I ran towards it, head down, using my weight to throw it back down the stair. There was a moment of contact between our bodies, and I felt as though a sharp, many toothed mouth had planted itself inside of my sternum and was churning away my flesh starting from the centre. I heard the body of my opponent clattering down the stairs as I fell backwards, clawing at my own skin, trying to get inside so that I could pull this feeling out.

It faded quickly, but not quickly enough. The companion of the first creature now stood above me. I kicked at it, then tried to roll out of the way, but it caught me and pinned me to the ground. Its stare burrowed into my eyes, like golden nails fixing my skull to the floor. Its mouth opened and I was swallowed whole.

I'd been so afraid of losing my nerve, but when the order had come I hadn't hesitated. A lot of my colleagues had seemed more afraid than I was.

To me, it seemed like no-man's land was a dream. Not even a dream. Dreams were more frightening.

The shell that got me, it wasn't even intended for me really. I'd only been injured because I had seen it coming, and I'd seen the pale, porridge-faced boy that it was coming for. I'd gotten in the way, protected him with my body instinctively, as if he were my child.

The bath was warm. I could feel the soft, black tendrils snaking up into my hair, gently massaging the edges of my skull as they burrowed into its dark recesses. There was no pain. I could feel the other dreamers in the water surrounding me. We were dreaming a new kingdom into existence. Somewhere, high above the sadistic stars, a malignant hunger was searching us out. I could feel it moving towards us, larval, unconscious, coming out of the darkness to seize its throne. Soon it would enshrine itself, a new god of war suited to a new age of slaughter.

I saw my dreams crystalizing into a landscape. When all had settled and hardened, and the new boundaries of the dream world had set, then it would devour us. It would imbibe a kind of intelligence from our ravaged minds. It would become a god, its fathomless will yoked to the logic of our nightmares. Perhaps if I could wake up... but there were so many dreamers who had seemed the same horrors. So many minds bringing the nightmare of reality into the world of dreams.

Post Scriptum

My sister was buried under a cross that bore my name, and the monument in town records that I gave my life for my country in 1916. Among the effects that were sent home was a small black book which once, in a moment of insanity, I bought from a peddler of occult wares. It had been empty at the time, but the man had assured me that it was of great value and tremendous antiquity. I should, therefore, have wondered why he was so eager to sell it and at such a small price. I suppose that on some level I believed it to be a worthless trinket, probably mass produced and artificially aged, and I bought it because it promised mystery to a life consumed by tedium.

Shortly after procuring it, I started to have the prophetic dream that haunted me throughout my youth. When the Great War broke out I was terrified by the rumours that came back to us from the front. Clearly the landscape of my dream had become a reality, and it was only a matter of time before my broken body would lay on a blighted stretch of foreign ground. It never occurred to me that it might have been someone else's body that I saw thrown across the sky.

When the book was returned to us, it was filled with the text that you read above. It was not written in my sister's hand. I fear that no earthly pen has ever touched its pages. It came to me, just as her letters had done, for that was the address that she had given. The rest I passed on to my mother. The book I kept, and I alone have read.

Whose Afraid of the Little Red Hood?

Red Riding Hood grew up mean. She'd go down to the meadow, picking flowers. When the wolves came she smiled and lured them to grandma's house. She killed them slow. You could hear the howling late into the night. Next morning, a bloodied daisy-chain hung above her door.

Last night, she came into the bar, sank her hatchet in the table, demanded ale. I loved the way the satin lining curled against her thigh. "Mind if I join you?"

She made room, but not conversation. We drank. She took me home.

This morning, a bloodied daisy-chain hangs above her bed.

Mother R'lyeh

"If cancer may attach itself to a body, thrive and ultimately claim the life of its host, why should Mother Earth be immune?" This remarkable statement was written on a scrap of paper sitting in the middle of an otherwise unremarkable coffee table. The table was oval, polished to a bright sheen with orange oil, covered with a cloth of handmade lace. Several copies of Reminisce magazine, a cinnamon scented candle, and a little pouch of floral fabric containing a pair of glasses were the only other objects that graced its surface.

"Very traditional." Brandee gave me a sidelong glance. Ze had been born my brother, and I had explained that Mrs. Verneer was extremely conservative, and would probably be alarmed by the cultivated androgyny that ze usually adopted in public. Out of respect for my client's sensitivities, my sib had dressed up very nicely in an almost schoolmarmish summer frock, with some cute Hello Kitty barrettes and a light dusting of modest make-up. "If it weren't for the illustration, one could imagine the text to be ordinary political alarmism. The 'cancer' could be anything from fracking to gay marriage. But..."

The 'illustration' was hard to explain. It was a twisting tangle of lines — almost the sort of thing that you might doodle absently if you were really angry. Yet it was different somehow. Figures and representations seemed to emerge from the incoherent graphite swirls, but before you could quite put your finger on what they were they would disappear again. Wherever you focused your attention, it was just meaningless scribbling, but you would have the sense that there was something climbing up out of the picture just a little to the left. "You're finding it unsettling too?"

"It isn't unsettling. It is unsettled." Brandee put it down on the table and brushed hir bangs back into place behind the left ear. "Does your friend usually show signs of paranoia?"

"Mrs. Verneer?" I gestured around the room. Several porcelain ladies blushingly dipped their parasols towards us from the shelves, and a ceramic cat grinned up over the top of a ball of pink wool. "What you see is what you get."

"What I see, at the moment is an empty cottage that is supposed to contain a very fragile shut-in with antedeluvian sensibilities and a sweet tooth. Can you think of anywhere that she might be?"

It was the question that we'd been trying to figure out when we had discovered the note on the table. To the best of my knowledge, the only time that Mrs. Verneer ever left her house was when I took her out. Today, Brandee had offered to come with me because it was the lady's birthday and Brandee had made her a heavenly variation on a traditional slagroomtaart — a frankly hideous name for a lovely dessert. "The hospital, maybe?" I suggested. "She seemed to be in good health on Wednesday, but sometimes..." I shrugged, trying to be professional about it.

Brandee wandered over the window and looked out into the drizzle. The yard must have been beautiful once, but my client's income had shrunk over the years and it had been some time since she'd been able to afford landscaping. In the spring I always helped her to plant a couple of dahlias in the front, and there was a "young lad" from down the road who came and cut the grass every couple of weeks, but the box hedges had become bulky and mishappen from neglect and a pernicious forest of hardy weeds had taken root in the front garden of the main house. "Who lives up there?"

"No one. It belongs to Mrs. Verneer, but she says it's too big to live in. This was the servants' cottage."

"Why hasn't she sold it?"

I shrugged. "Sentiment, I guess."

"You said she has no children."

"She had three. But none surviving."

"Why keep a big old house like that if you've got no one to leave it to? Sentiment won't answer for it. Look. She's the kind of woman who cares whether the napkins match the tea-cups. She'd rather have the house lived in by someone who could afford to keep it up than hold on to it and watch it decay. I don't like it. It doesn't scan."

I sat down on the sofa and tried not to roll my eyes. "Real people are complicated. In real life, you can't figure out everything about a person from their bookshelf and the scratches on their cell-phone."

My sib looked at me archly. "I know that. A single variation on theme is just personality. Two, eccentricity. But three signifies. And today, there are three. A note on the table. A house that ought to have been sold years ago. And a woman who can't leave her lazy-boy without assistance has vanished."

"Probably she called 911."

"No. Look at the drive. Yours are the only tracks. An ambulance is a very heavy vehicle, it has a wide and distinctive footprint. The mud remembers you being here on Wednesday. It doesn't remember anybody else."

I joined my sibling at the window and followed hir finger as it traced the line that my wheels had traced on the muddy drive. I didn't like melodrama, and it especially irked me when it turned out to be perfectly reasonable. "Okay." I paced up and down the small cottage, my brain churning through various impossibilities. I even looked in the broom closet.

"I doubt a respectable 87 year old woman is playing hide-and-seek," Brandee chided me. "Come on. We're going to go up to the house."

"Lived in." Brandee declared as we mounted the step onto the front porch. It certainly wasn't the first thing I would have concluded. It was clearly a very long time since anybody had done any housekeeping. An elaborate spider web spanned the distance from the posts to the brick wall, a recently entangled fly lay exhausted in its netting, occasionally buzzing as it tried to wriggle free. The remnants of older webs fluttered from the eaves. The windows were begrimed with dust and several of the small, square panes were broken.

"No one lives here."

"There is a recent pattern of wear on the steps, suggesting occupation or at the very least frequent use."

I rolled my eyes and sighed. "Brandee, you're a baker, not a detective. How on earth can you tell when the steps got worn."

"Look. When someone walks repeatedly over an old wooden step the paint flakes off, the wood is exposed and it starts being worn down. Like this," ze indicated. "If that had happened fifty years ago then the exposed wood would be grey and mildewy, like this," a weathered ballustrade illustrated the point, "but it's not. I don't have to be a detective to have the use of simple reason."

I put my hands on my hips to look as if I was still unconvinced. I'd asked Brandee once why, being so smart, ze'd gone into pastries. Hir reply was that cakes make people happy, while philosophy only makes them confused. "You know," I said. "If it is being lived in probably we don't want to meet the people who are living in it. Squatters tend to be addicts."

"Your old lady lives right there. Her chair looks out of that window, and she is unable to leave that chair. Whomever lives here goes freely up and down these stairs. Ergo, not squatting."

"Mrs. Verneer wouldn't know. She's almost completely blind."

I could see that Brandee hadn't considered this, and I felt a little victorious. "Deaf?" ze asked.

"Mostly."

"I see. You should have said. It puts a very different complexion on things."

"I did say. Just now. This is the first that it's come up."

"All right." Ze pushed open the door. The old springs creaked like a wounded bird. Ze reached into the darkness and hir hand re-emerged bearing an old-fashioned cane topped by a sharp-tailed ivory dragon. "We'll go carefully. And I'll go first." Hir foot fell on the threshold.

"I have a better idea. We call the police." I'd seen very few horror movies, most of them when I was a teenager. I couldn't stand the genre, mostly because people did evidently stupid things when all they really needed to do was call on competent authorities.

"You have no sense of fun. But if you must know, we're not getting reception. I imagine it's some combination of the hills and the weather."

"There's a landline in the cottage."

"All right then, you go call the police. It'll take them at least fifteen minutes to get out here. In the meantime, I'm going to investigate."

"Why? Its dangerous, and you're not qualified."

"Alana, the people in horror movies are not stupid." Brandee often said things that gave the impression that ze could read minds. It had always creeped me out. "They're human. Even if they don't admit it to themselves, they know that they are probably only going to get one chance in life to be involved in something truly dreadful, mysterious and interesting. If they pass it up, they'll be safe. And safety is boring."

I guess I'm boring. I went back to the cottage, figuring that Brandee wouldn't be able to get into too much trouble in the time it would take me to call 911. Also figuring that if ze did get into trouble, I was likely to be more of a liability than a help. If there was a fight, I would so turn out to be one of those girls who shrieks and occasionally throws a shoe into the fray. I knew it.

I dialed. The phone rang a couple of times and I heard someone pick up, but I couldn't tell what they were saying. Their voice came out like the sound of a violin bow being drawn across splintered bone – including the god-awful shrieks that you would expect a person to make under such circumstances. "Hello," I said. The shrieking pitched into a lower register, like something moaning in unholy labour. I hung up, tried again. This time there was an explosion of frenzied howling with metallic strings harping sinister hymns in the background. I felt violated by the sound. I slammed the phone back into its cradle and curled up for a moment in the lazy boy, feeling sick.

Trying to regain my equilibrium, I picked up a glass of water that had been left on the chair-side table. It had been resting atop a small photo album, the kind with a brown plastic cover and an oval window in the front. The window showed a picture of the house at the top of the hill. For a moment, it looked like there was a figure on the porch but when I picked it up to get a better look the figure was gone. I could still feel it, though, as if it had ducked aside and was peering at me from around the edges of the album cover. I opened the album. The pictures inside were the same. They looked superficially ordinary: pictures taken when Mrs. Verneer had been a younger woman, perhaps in her fifties. In some of them she was gardening, showing off a bed of daffodils, or hosting a party on the lawn with people who I didn't recognize. Yet everytime that I flipped to a new photograph I had the sense that someone was creeping out of view, hiding behind a tree, ducking in behind a group of children, fleeing for the edges of the picture.

As I progressed through the album, the pictures themselves began to change. At first it was just that the expressions seemed to become unhappier, the weather more overcast. By the mid-point no one was happy anymore. Mrs. Verneer looked up from a bed of wilting flowers with hollow eyes that stared relentlessly into the camera. A group of middle-aged men huddled under an awning, clutching their beers with white knuckles, peering at me in stark desperation. Things were moving in the shadows of the trees behind them and a steady rain began to wash over the face of the photos, shimmering with a faintly oily texture. I flipped to the end. The final image wasn't a photograph at all. It was a dissolved landscape, with impossible textures and sickening angles. The rain had settled into pools. They were not red, but they gave the impression of being blood or some mixture of obscene bodily fluids. A yawning distortion suggested a gaping birth canal from which something vile was struggling to emerge.

I closed the book, gulped down the water. Nausea was no longer an excuse. With my legs trembling beneath me, I staggered towards the door.

Step one: get Brandee.
Step two: get in the car.

Step three: get out of here.
Step four: get help.

I wasn't sure what kind of help you called on in this sort of emergency. It felt like it would be vaguely irresponsible to call a group of local police to the scene, especially since they would they would casually disregard my description of the dangers, but I didn't have the number for the Ghostbusters. An exorcist maybe? I tried to imagine Father Jacob's reaction to my phone call. I doubted the diocese even had an exorcist anymore.

Sometimes forethought is a defense mechanism. I was imagining problems in the far future to avoid thinking about the fact that I hadn't even managed to accomplish step one. A piercing sound, somewhere between a battle cry and a scream, snapped me back to reality. I ran towards it.

It came from a sheltered courtyard in the middle of the house. Coming out of the ground, from the centre of a tangled mass of overgrown rose-bushes, was a thing. It was about thirteen feet tall. If I were to describe it with ordinary nouns they would be words like "tree" "snake" "fish" "umbilical cord." Bark-like scales clung to a fleshy body of pulsating vessels. Sharp fins whistled through the air as a twisted maw darted towards Brandee, who was on the ground in front of it. The Victorian cane was thrust into a rose-bush several feet away and ze was beating the thing vigorously with one of hir high heels.

I ducked in, retrieved the cane, and swung it towards a pulsing bulge that looked vaguely like an eye. The ivory dragon's tail sank in deep, and a thick, purple-green sap spurted into the air. The ground beneath me began to heave and tremble as the roots of the creature twisted in pain. It thrashed blindly towards me, and I didn't even feel anything as one of its fins sliced into my arm. I swung again. My second blow glanced off of its armoured body. The third struck. The head of the cane buried itself between two of the creature's scales. As it contorted, the scales embraced the weapon so tightly that I couldn't pull it free. I was thrown to the ground and the cane snapped, leaving me with a splintered stick not more than two feet long.

It lunged towards me, several ranks of teeth glinting out from blackened, superating gums. I parried. The splintered end of the broken cane drove into its head, just beneath the twisting jaw. As its massive body began to writhe, the ground cracked open and a bloodied root grasped at me from the broken soil.

The creature fell. Its weight crashed down on my pelvis, pinning me in place. Beneath the ground there was a final spasm and then it was still.

I stared up at the sky. Stupid thoughts go through your head in situations like this. In this case, "Oh my God. I didn't shriek."

When I raised my head I could see Brandee hacking with a rusted garden spade at a fleshy tendril that had twined itself around hir ankle. Ze looked a mess. "Are you hurt?" I asked.

"No." The spade cut through the last of the fibrous tissue. My sibling stood, brushing the dirt and dead leaves from hir dress. A grimace tightened hir features as ze took a step. "I think the ankle might swell. But nothing serious. Nothing like *that*."

Like I said before, I hadn't even noticed when it cut me. Now I followed Brandee's finger towards my own left arm. The flesh was deeply torn and a severed artery was leaching blood onto the soil. I felt suddenly cold. "I think I-I'm going into shock," I stuttered.

"What do I do?"

My body began to shiver, my teeth chattering violently. "Th-th-the-the-there's a m-m-medical k-kit in the car. A-a-a-and an emergenc-c-cy blanket."

Brandee limped towards the door.

"W-w-w-wait." I said. "Give me y-y-y-your pantyhose."

Ze winced as ze worked them over hir injured ankle. They were badly torn and stained with the creature's blood, but I didn't need them to be pretty.

I tied as tight a tourniquet as I could manage with one hand and then held myself up, half-sitting, refusing to pass out.

"I made it." From Brandee's tone, I didn't get the impression that making it out to the car and back had been a pleasant country walk. An old umbrella was serving as a walking cane, and the shaft had become substantially warped by hir weight. Ze put the medical kit on the ground and spread the blanket over me, tucking me in. "I also found this." A large wrench that I used for changing tires. "I didn't get attacked by anything, but the earth is definitely not happy. The ground out there is like an ocean before a storm."

I reached over and clicked a small metal button in the corner of the blanket. The button catalyzed a chemical reaction in a gel layer inside of the blanket. It became stiff, heavy feeling, and a slow wave of warmth began to creep over my body. It was a good blanket. My teeth stopped clattering. "I'm going to need suture, and a needle, and a shot of morphine." As the adrenaline left my system, I was starting to feel pain. I didn't want to think about what Brandee was saying. I wanted to think that this was over, that I had been victorious, that we'd survived.

Brandee made a remarkably competent nurse. I was less sure of myself as a surgeon. Obviously I'd done sutures before, but with a severed artery it's a lot more complicated than just stitching up the epidermis. Also, I was feeling pretty dizzy from the blood loss and even though I hadn't taken very much morphine it also served to blunt my senses. I did the best I could. "I need to get to a hospital. That should hold okay, but it may continue to bleed internally."

Brandee unhooked a bird-feeder from an old iron post and wrenched it out of the ground, using it as a lever to lift the weight of the dead thing from off of me. I wriggled free. My hips felt sore and bruised but not seriously injured. I twined my good arm around my sibling and we leaned on each other, providing mutual support. "I think I've had enough fun," Brandee quipped. "Let's go."

The first time through, I'd been running and hadn't bothered to take a look at the interior of the house. It was like you might imagine an exhibit in a museum to be twenty years after the zombie apocalypse. None of the furnishings had seen much actual use, and it was obvious that they had all been very expensive and very modern in the '70s. Although the exterior of the house retained its fin de siecle charm, the interior was a celebration of leather and crome, stark colours and irregular shapes. There was even a lava-lamp — not the usual conical kind that you find in grimcrack stores, but an elaborate hand-blown creation made of tiered glass bubbles. Everything was covered with dust and cobwebs. One of the sofas had its taut, cream leather surface torn open in a ragged slash. Another was lightly speckled with dried blood.

"I didn't like it either," Brandee observed. "It looks too staged. Like the inhabitant is putting on a halloween production for intrusive urchins."

"I also can't imagine Mrs. Verneer picking out this funiture."

"People get funny when they get old. They may be quite fashion conscious in their youth, and then suddenly one day they wake up with a craving for doilies."

The talk was a distraction. It made us feel normal, I guess. It stopped when we entered the front room.

Through the window my car was clearly visible, hanging about thirty feet up in the air from the branches of a tree that clearly hadn't been there ten minutes ago. A long, silvery limb has thrust itself through the passenger window and out of the windshield. The limb attached to a trunk that looked almost more like stone than bark. A second tree had grown alongside it on the other side of the drive, and high overhead they had joined their limbs together to create a dark archway. Had it not been for a couple of leaden-looking leaves that hung from the ends of sculpted branches I would have described the trees as architectural rather than natural features.

"All right," Brandee's voice always falls by half an octave when ze's in a crisis. "We'll stay inside and we'll wait. It's a good thing you called the police. I apologize for twitting you about it."

I sat down heavily on chair that had been designed to curve like a reclining fashion model. "I tried to call. I didn't succeed." I quickly outlined my excursion to the cottage.

"I see. In that case," Brandee said calmly, "I think we're fucked." Ze crossed the room to where a bar curved lazily along the corner. From behind it ze produced several crystal decanters. The surfaces were cloudy, but the interiors contained several different shades of amber liquids.

"What are you doing?"

"I'm having a drink. You're having one too." Ze opened one and smelled it, blinking at the odor. "Definitely still potent." Pouring the stuff out into wine glasses, ze handed me one and downed the other.

"So our plan is palliative care through alcoholism?"

"No. Our plan is to figure out who lives here, and what they've been doing. You can see easily enough where the dust has been disturbed. There are two trails. One goes to the courtyard, which we've already seen. We're going to follow the other one as soon as you've finished your draught of courage."

The steps led down into the basement. You expect crazy people to write disturbing messages on doors and walls, either scratched in with a sharp implement or inscribed in blood. You don't expect needlepoint.

It was a framed oval covered in a sheet of fractured glass. The stitches were reminiscent of the illustration and the photographs: the same sickening lines, except that the three dimensional medium seemed to more fully convey the horror of the image. When you looked at it, you became immediately aware that the threads were constantly crossing over one another, obscuring the thread beneath, and that the whole mass was completely covering up the embroidery cloth below. It gave the sense that anything, literally anything, could be hidden there. I pulled it off the wall and turned it over, using a pair of scissors I cut the threads from the back and laid bare the cloth.

On it were written the words "Mother Time, pregnant with the End. Mother Time in whom Eternity is swallowed. Mother Time, bring forth your son." Beneath this something further was scribbled in a script that I couldn't read.

Brandee reached into hir pocket and withdrew the note that we had taken from Mrs. Verneer's table. Ze turned it over and slowly rubbed the side of a pencil across the back of it. "Something was written here too," ze said, "before it was scribbled over. Give me a moment, it's hard to make out." I waited as ze mouthed words to herself.

"What does it say?"

"Something like, 'O Womb of the Restless Dreamer. O City most Dead. O Breeder of Aeons, bring forth your son. Then there's more of that gibberish."

"It's just crazy talk. Schizophrenics write stuff like that."

"It maketh the earth to quake and bring forth unnatural issue. Otherwise, I would agree."

I was well beyond insisting that there had to be a rational explanation. I opened the basement door.

It wasn't a basement. It was as if the foundation of the house was the entirety of time and space reduced to a pile of rubble, encroached upon by some unfathomable primordial void. I felt as if my mind was utterly violated by it, and then as if the products of that violation were being scraped out by a sharp currette.

When I regained myself, Brandee had me by the waist. The door had been slammed shut and ze was leaning again it, breathing as if at the end of a long struggle. I pried myself free and slumped beside hir on the floor. "It isn't a place," I said.

"What isn't a place?"

"The City of the Old Ones. It's not a place. It's their mother. It doesn't matter where. Anywhere the Seed falls, R'Lyeh is."

"Alana..."

I pushed my hands down into the floor. I could feel the power growing inside my body. I understood. My mind had been prepared. Mrs. Verneer's also, I was sure. Stripped of self, identity and conscience I was no longer I. Soon my arms would reach up towards the sky and form an archway through which my son might one day crawl. Strange words, untranslatable, poured from my lips in an ecstasy. I called upon my sisters, who would come to dream the dreamer into being.

The wrench came down so quickly, and with such force, that I didn't even have time to feel the pain.

When I awoke I was perched on the back of a lawnmower, tied with strong ropes, cruising down the road a breezy five kilometres per hour. Brandee was driving. Behind us, I could see the archway that rose up above the treeline over Mrs. Verneer's house. It stirred in me a longing more painful than grief, but I had been bound so tightly that my struggling barely amounted to more than a pitiful winding, like a worm on a hook.

I was committed to a hospital for several months, sunk in a depression so deep that I was hardly able to swallow. Eventually I started to eat again, and nowadays, occasionally, I speak. Brandee tells me nothing about whatever happened when I was unconscious, but I can see it there, eating away behind hir eyes. Ze also saw into that door, just a glimpse, and ze knows that yearning for death-in-life, beyond eternity. Hir mind saw it, but ze dragged me away out of jealousy, because hir body could not bring it forth.

Of course ze denies it. The only explanation ze gives is, "You're my sister. One day that will be enough to explain everything. And when it does, that's how I'll know that you're yourself again."

BUFFALO TONGUE WOMAN

There was a man who had a nagging wife. She was always complaining: he did not bring enough meat home from the hunt, he did not win enough victories in battle, he did not give her children, his penis was too small. Sometimes she said these things to the other women in the village, and they would laugh at him. His wife's name was Buffalo Tongue Woman.

One day, he was coming home with some meat for his woman to dry. When he got to the door of the tent she started to complain about what he had brought. It was not enough. The other wives always got better than she did. Nearby, there was a young beautiful girl, not yet married, braiding her hair. When that young girl heard what Buffalo Tongue Woman said, she covered her mouth and laughed.

The man went inside the tent. He took out his knife and held Buffalo Tongue Woman down on the ground, so he could cut the tongue out of her mouth. Then he hung it up to dry and he told her, "I have won a great victory." He told everyone else that Raven had come in the night and eaten the tongue out of her mouth because she had offended the spirits.

After that, Buffalo Tongue Woman started to become very sick because she could not speak. After a while, she was with child, but she was too weak for giving birth. The child came early. For three days and nights, Buffalo Tongue Woman was in labor with that child. Her cries were very terrible to hear because there was no tongue in her mouth. It made her sound like an animal. The cries disturbed everyone in the camp, and they whispered about how probably she had gotten with child by a bear spirit to be making such a racket. After the third day, she died. The midwife had to reach inside of her to pull the baby out, and when it was born it was very small and blue.

The child did not die. But by her fourth summer, she still had not spoken a word. The people named her No Tongue Girl. The man was afraid that the spirits were punishing him by making his daughter mute.

He went out into the darkness and made a tobacco offering, and then Coyote came. There was a buffalo lying on the ground, and it had died of a disease. There were many flies living in its carcass. Coyote went over and pulled the tongue out of the dead buffalo's head. The tongue was half rotten, but Coyote ate it. Then the man knew that he had to feed the mother's tongue to the girl, and this would make her able to speak.

The tongue was very old by this time, and there was only a little piece left, all shriveled up. The man put it into a mortar and pestle and ground it up and mixed it with a little fat to disguise the taste. Then he fed the tongue to his girl.

So now she could speak. At first, the man was very happy, and he told how his daughter had been cured by Coyote. The girl could not only speak, but she spoke like a bird in the forest, that makes delight in the heart of everyone who hears it. She had nothing but praise for everything. But during the night, when the girl was asleep, her mothers dead tongue awoke in her throat. It told lies. It said, "Your daughter speaks to flatter when you are here, but when you are gone she tells everyone how you are worthless." The man tried to stop up his ears, but soon he started to believe what the tongue was saying.

One night, he could endure no more. He seized his daughter by her hair and held her down on the floor. He cut the tongue out of her mouth. But this time the blood went down into her throat as she was screaming, and it choked her. She was coughing and coughing, but the blood had turned into a solid lump and she could not get it out. The breath left her body and she died.

The man was very afraid. He put the body in the river and told everyone that she had drowned. But he had forgotten about the tongue, which was still in his tent.

While he was gone, some vultures came and they ate the tongue that was lying in the tent. They started to fly around the village saying to everyone, "My father cut out my mother's tongue and killed her, and he cut out my tongue and killed me." Everyone knew who they were talking about. They tied the man up for the animals to come and eat and they moved their village, because this thing, when a father had killed his child, was the worst thing that could happen. They could no longer live in this place.

So the man was tied up with sinews. He could not get his hands free. He tried until his blood came out, and the smell of it brought many animals. Coyote came first of all. He had known what was going to happen when he showed the man how to give speech to his daughter. Now he began to eat the man's leg.

Some of the blood from the tongue had gone down into the ground, and from that place a plant grew, shaped like many sharp tongues. It spoke to the man in the voice of his wife, taunting him for being too weak to escape, and laughing at how it had made him kill his daughter. The plant would not be silent, and when the man finally died more of those same plants grew up out of his body. So probably those tongues are still speaking the same way to him now that he is dead.

Against Nature

"I have decided to utterly reject nature." Andre was sitting on the corner of a love-seat that had lost its left arm, his hand bent elaborately behind his back like a horror-movie magician about to pull an eviscerated rabbit out of thin air.

"Which kind of nature?" I asked absently, looking up from a dense passage of *Metaphysics of Morals*.

"All of them. Nature," he continued, "is the universal religion of mankind. It is our obsession. Our Golden Calf. On the left, or on the right. With the Catholics, it's always "natural law" and "natural family planning" and "sins against nature." With the Lefties it's "natural fibers", "natural child-birth" and "natural medicine." Environmentalists deprive us of whale meat and forbid Brazilian peasants their livelihood. Why? Because they want to save "Nature." Humanists babble about the "natural rights of man." Scientists are always searching for the "laws of nature." The old pagans sacrificed their children to Mother Nature. The psycho-analysts worship "human nature." Even the pederasts claim that they must have their catamites, because for them, it is perfectly "natural." So I say I won't have it. I abhor nature and I spit in her face with all the venom of my aching soul."

"You missed Wall Street."

He looked annoyed and continued as though I hadn't spoken. "I'm going to start a movement. The anti-naturalists."

"You could all wear T-shirts that say 'Rise up against gravity.'"

"Scoff," he sniffed. With a baleful sigh, he groped in his pocket and withdrew a dollar-store cigarette case. Apart from a pack of nicotine-stained rolling papers it was empty. He started rummaging around in the ash-tray for butt ends that still had a few flakes of spittly tobacco hanging from them. "I have been ruminating over the matter for several days. The problem is to come up with a new way of living; something that eschews nature in all of her guises. A true breach with the essence of the human heart."

"You could pluck out your eyes and have them replaced with mechanical implants," I suggested. "If you want, I've got a miniature ice-cream scoop that's about the right size. We could do it right now in the kitchen."

"Don't be banal. What I need is an inspiration, a dark muse to descend and tempt me with a sin such as has never been committed before. A sin against everything. Yes. That's it precisely."

"Mmm. Are you going to patent it? You wouldn't want a bunch of posers running around committing your sin."

He had managed to find a cigarette end and was struggling to light it with a pack of matches that someone had spilled rum on the night before. By the time that the match was lit, the tiny clump of pre-charred tobacco had fallen out of the paper and scattered itself across the ruffles of his blouse. "I'm going to the store," he declared grandly. "You should think about what I've said to you. It is not often that you have the privilege of learning the secret of true freedom." Putting on his coat, he picked up the decorative sword-stick for which, one of these days, he was sure to get arrested. As the door clattered behind him I wondered whether you could reasonably universalize the maxim that pretentious nihilism be punishable by hanging.

"Eating your own unborn child," Andre had not let go of the issue and was running through a litany of evils that he thought might not have been tried previously.

"Caligula," I replied. "Impregnated his sister because he thought he was Zeus. Ate his child so that it could pop fully formed out of his head."

"Deliberately concocting a virulent disease."

"United States Patent 4,647,773."

"Gluttony. That's it. There has to be a capital sin of gluttony, and I'm going to be the one to find it."

"Apicius. Ancient Roman gourmand. Committed suicide because he could no longer afford fried flamingo tongues."

"Burning down a national monument just because it's a monument. A deliberate act of cultural destruction."

"Everybody's done that."

"I could invent a time machine, go back, and prevent nature from ever coming into existence in the first place."

"Like the Master in Dr. Who?"

"What about endangered species? I could hunt a species to extinction not because I wanted its skin, horns, or meat, but just to have been the one to have shot the last Siberian Tiger."

"Go for it! Give some Siberian Tiger the satisfaction of eating the only man who knows the secret of true freedom."

"Genius is such a burden," he lamented. "I'm going to make myself something to eat."

"You should eat a Mr. Noodle with Cheez Whiz. That's an abomination against nature if ever there was one."

The week-end had come and gone. I had finished Kant and was procrastinating on my philosophy paper by re-watching the entire series of Twin Peaks. It had a lot of very creepy images of nature and a number of interesting sins, but nothing that hadn't been committed before. I had heard that the originator of the series used to make jig-saw puzzles from dead animals, which might have qualified, but Andre wanted a sin of his own; he wouldn't be content to bite David Lynch's style. Andre had just run up another three hundred dollars of credit-card debt on a smoking jacket that he had seen in the window of an import clothing store. It had embroidered pea-cocks vying with one another on the lapels, and a red sash that didn't quite cinch in properly around Andre's anorexic hips. He was standing in front of a mirror and admiring himself while sipping a glass of obscenely cheap fortified wine.

"Have you come up with a new sin yet?" I asked.

"I have changed my criteria. Having thought on it I realized that everyone is coming up with new sins these days. Think about recycling. Twenty years ago, throwing your trash in the bin was the civilized thing to do. Now it's a sin if you don't separate your cans and bottles. Pish. And of course there are test-tube babies. Even you can't come up with an ancient Roman who made test-tube babies. That's a completely twentieth century sin. All of that is old. I've decided to come up with a sin against myself. Against my own philosophy. Against the natural human drive to believe what we think is actually true. I am going to convince myself of something that I know to be a lie."

"So you're going to hire a phone psychic."

He ignored me. "A sin against my sense of intellectual self-preservation. Yes!" A bizarre, almost mystic light came into his eyes, and even his goat-piss sherry suddenly glinted in his hand as though it was made of liquid amber. "I'm going to get myself murdered. Not just murdered. Violently tortured, then murdered. I am going to become the first martyr of nihilism!" He stood back and examined himself in the mirror. "I'll be martyred in this very jacket just to add poignancy to the act."

I did not expect him to take himself seriously.

I arrived home after a day of reading old French poets and scanning philosophy journals for articles on anti-naturalism. If I could prove to Andre that his idea had been around since the nineteenth century, he would drop it like a moldy potato and start searching for a more "original" philosophy. There were three police cars in front of our house. An officer stopped me at the door and demanded to know if I lived there, when I had seen Andre last, and what I had been doing this afternoon. He searched through my pockets and back-pack, then stole my coat to run laboratory tests on it. Several impositions on my personal and civil rights later, in frustration, I began quoting Voltaire and Locke at him. I think this convinced him that I was a dangerous agitator. He wrote copiously in his notebook and instructed me that I was not to leave the area for any reason.

For a long time I sat on a sofa while the po rifled through Andre's indie comics and scrutinized the absurd "literary diary" that he kept for posthumous publication. Eventually, through pestering and subterfuge, I discovered what had happened: Andre had not been tortured to death or gloriously mutilated for his lack of cause. He had gone wandering around one of the gloomier ends of town, presumably relishing the thought of joining a terrorist cell so that the CIA would be compelled to bathe his eyeballs in sulfuric acid, and had been beaten and robbed. I had little doubt that this was against his nihilistic will — a common bandit killing him for his maxed-out credit card and aluminum cigarette case would have been an insult to his ontological dignity.

Andre's face was pale and bruised, like one of those Victorian crucifixions where Christ looks like a consumptive girl. A heart-monitor bleeped melodramatically nearby. The smoking jacket — almost certainly the cause of his ill-fortune — was conspicuously absent. Presumably the mugger could not believe that someone in such a coat had only fifty-two cents to his name.

Andre's mother stood next to the bed, holding his hand and chanting some Hinduesque mantra. I was sure that it was a Western smarmy-swami forgery. She had invited me along out of some notion that I was like a brother to her son, and possibly in the delusion that we were lovers. Andre never took girls home because it made him look predictable. His mother — an aging dilettante with dyed-black hair and a degree in psychology -- was old enough to think that ruffled shirts and a theatrical personality were sure signs of an alternate sexual trajectory and modern enough to be self-consciously open-minded about it.

For a while she hovered around pestering the doctors about her son's condition before finally going downstairs to buy some of that white gunge that lurks in hospital cafeterias under the assumed name of Vanilla Pudding.

"Has she departed?" Andre opened his eyes. "I didn't want to talk to her. She wouldn't be capable of understanding."

"Understanding what?"

"That I did it." He leaned his head up a little, which made several of the monitors beep in alarm. As the nurse rushed in he dropped back down and played dead.

"Did he say something?"

"He's awake," I explained "just pretending to be unconscious so he doesn't have to talk to his mom." She tapped at Andrew's hollow cheeks, pulled open his eyes, called his name, then contemplated referring me to psyche ward before returning to her desk.

Andrew's eyes opened and he smiled like the Cheshire cat.

"What is it that you've done, exactly?" I asked.

"Why, I've become a martyr. The first martyr of the anti-naturalists!"

I didn't mention that there was another philosophic movement that had already claimed this name. It didn't seem the place. "The difficulty I see with your theory, is that you're not dead. Martyrs don't generally get to gloat over their victory."

"I was dead," he explained calmly. "In dying by my own will, without the impetus of suffering or despair, for no reason except to spit in the face of nature, I have become anti-nature. Death is a natural process. Don't you see what that means?"

"That you have a concussion?"

"I am exempt from death. I have wrested the flaming sword from the hands of the angel who stands guardian over paradise. I have eaten from the Tree of Life. I have made my own immortality."

"By getting biffed by a mugger?"

"Not a common mugger. A manifestation of my will. He wasn't real. He was Nature in all her brutal imbecility, summoned into being by my defiance. I banished him from existence at the moment of my death."

"And this figment of your will just happened to steal your credit card and jacket?"

"I hear my mother coming. Please don't tell her any of this. It is quite beyond her."

They kept Andrew in the hospital overnight. When the police came to ask questions he answered sensibly enough, saying that his assailant was nearly as tall as a hill-giant, excruciatingly ugly, with an obscenely denuded head, and several hideous growths around the eyes. The police sketch artist managed to produce from this an incredible likeness of a human being. Andrew admitted that, apart from the lack of feral teeth and the needless introduction of some symmetry in the features, it was a good representation. Since I could not possibly be construed to resemble the attacker and Andrew seemed to be on friendly terms with me, I was informed I could resume moving about as I pleased.

His mother lurked about our house for a day before excusing herself. She left a multitude of phone numbers where she could be reached, and plenty of cash in case Andrew needed anything. I informed all of my professors that my assignments would be late on account of a violent incident that had left me terribly rattled and unable to understand Heidegger.

With his mother gone, Andrew declared that he was no longer enduring the importunities of mortals. He retreated to his room and locked the door. After several hours, I wisely discerned that what he really needed to restore him to health and sanity was a thirteen course Indian feast. I had this delivered and was soon munching on a poppadom, confident that sooner or later the scent of rogan josh and saag paneer would lure him from his lair.

Perhaps he had conquered nature and mortality, but I could not believe that he had conquered curry.

I ate deeply, and was leafing through The Brother's Karamazov, when I heard a loud clatter from his room. I pounded on the door. No answer. I addressed its stubborn silence with my shoulder-blade. This was not so successful as it is in crime dramas. Collapsing on the floor of the hall, I nursed my bruised shoulder and wondered if I should call the landlord.

Andrew opened the door and looked at me nonchalantly, as though he had no part in my current humiliation. He was wearing his smoking jacket.

I stared at him for a moment. I was sure that the jacket had not been in his room -- I had described it to the police, and they had not included it in their inventory. Andrew must have hidden it away in the bottom of one of his drawers before going out the other night.

He walked past me and seated himself in the living room, looking out past the faded mustard-green curtains that were fraying in the front window.

"How are you feeling?" I asked.

He didn't answer me. The bruises on his face were still very dark -- almost blacker than when he had been hospitalized. At length he said, "Theodore. Do you think that I'm insane?"

"I think that you've been injured."

"You mean that I am insane, but it will only be a temporary matter. Very well. That is understandable. I would not believe you if you were to say to me the things that I have said to you. Not that you would ever have thought of them. Poets and philosophers are dreamers. They never actually accomplish anything." He resumed looking out the window, and it was no longer possible to engage him in conversation. I returned to Dostoevsky, and when I was ready to go to bed, I tried to move him back into his room. He pushed me away, and continued to stare at the street-lit fog of the very early morning. I put a mountain of tandoori chicken on a plate, poured a glass of stale red wine, left it out for him, then went to bed.

I started the next morning with my customary breakfast: one cup of coffee, one cigarette. I sat down in the sagging, broken, red-upholstered arm chair, and was about to file some hysterical "final notices" in the wastebin, when I noticed that something was amiss in the backyard. Ordinarily it was a little patch of ill-tended lawn cramped between the overgrown clematis hugging the fence and the rusted shed full of spiders in the corner. Today it was a field of dusty gray broken occasionally by a ripple of bright blue. It took me several minutes to realize that the slightly shifting carpet was composed entirely of butterflies.

"Karner Blues," Andrew had come into the room behind me. He took the cigarette out of my hand, which had gone slightly limp in surprise at the infestation of lovely lycaeidae spreading their wings out on my yard. "They're nearly extinct, you know. They don't live in this area, of course. Pine barrens, I believe, though of course I only found all of this out last night myself. They had to fly all night to get here."

"What are you talking about?"

He smiled with awful self-satisfaction. The butterflies, all at once, rose up in a blue cloud that hovered at about my height over the yard. I felt keenly the tragedy of being unable capture this host of butterflies in a net of words as Wordsworth had netted his daffodils. Several of them landed on the window and I could see their delicate feet crawling along the glass.

It was several minutes before I realized that there was a strange sound accompanying the insects, and several seconds more for me to identify it as the shrill cry of blackbirds. They descended on the butterflies, clawing at each others eyes and wings in their furious hunger for the feast. In minutes, there was not a single insect remaining alive. "And now," said Andrew, "they *are* extinct. They were Nabokov's favorite."

The blackbirds, one by one, started falling out of the sky and landing in the backyard, their talons clawing at the air, flapping pitifully as the wings from their half-consumed prey broke from their beaks and fluttered to the ground around them. Apparently the butterflies were poisonous.

"Andre?" I pushed open the door to his room.

"You've come to reprove me."

"Yes. I mean...This is going to sound stupid..." I couldn't get it out. It was too stupid.

"You don't want me to strip Nature's bounty of any more of it's gems?"

"Please don't."

"Theodore, tell me. What is your favorite species?"

"Look, I'm going to go out and clean up the backyard."

"By which you mean that you expect me to deliberately destroy your favorite, simply as an act of cruelty. On the contrary. Friendship is a most unnatural commodity. Natural man is always fighting with man, grubbing and grasping for his own bit of land, his own job, his own woman. Natural man is obscene and vulgar. Our friendship is not vulgar."

"I'm glad to hear that. Promise me, then, that you won't do that again."

"A weighty matter. I promise that I will take it under serious consideration in honor of the affection that I hold you in. I swear," he paused, contemplating the question of what deity deserved to act as surety for his word, "by myself."

I spent the afternoon with my face wrapped in a cloth soaked with vinegary wine, and my hand protected by a plastic shopping bag as I filled garbage sacks with dead birds. The flies had gathered so thickly that I could hardly see.

When I finished it was dark. Andre had gone out. I collapsed on the couch and spent the evening trying to map out an equilateral triangle amongst the stalactites of stucco on the ceiling. Andre arrived home after midnight. I asked him where he had been.

"Immortality amongst mortals is a tedious business," he replied. "I have been petitioning."

"Petitioning whom?"

"It took me the better part of the afternoon. I have searched out all of the Pantheons. The Germanic gods are altogether too obsessed with the natural, and the monotheists won't broke competition. The Norse are utterly barbaric, practically beasts. The Egyptians are insane. The Aztecs blood-thirsty. And the Hindu gods have too many arms. I've decided on the Greeks. They, at least, are civilized."

"I see."

"Scoff if you must," he said. "I think that I shall be going to bed."

This became the pattern of our days. Every morning he would slaughter an innocent species, taking impish delight at the catastrophic vicissitudes of nature gone awry. In honor of my request he would no longer actually destroy the entire species: he always left two, a male and a female, to go forth into the world and multiply. I tried to explain to him about genetic diversity but he would simply say that if they had been willing to do it for Noah, they would do it for him.

While I was cleaning up the back he would disappear until sometime around midnight. After four days of this I looked at the sea of torn, upturned white bellies and sleek, green spotted legs splayed in our backyard -- the remnants of a sub-species of frogs -- and decided that I didn't have time to clean up after him anymore. It was impossible to go to the police: what would I say? My room-mate fancies himself a minor, latter-day Caligula, and he happens to have the god-like powers to support his claims? I called my landlord and left a message on the machine: "Dead frogs in backyard. Better switch lawn care companies."

The day outside was dismal, overhung with low fog and an occasional touch of drizzle. Andre emerged from his room, went to the kitchen, and came out with a jar of honey and a bottle of wine. He appeared surprised that I wasn't outside, and quickly stashed his repast in the inner pockets of his coat. He flung the door open with needless zeal and stepped out into the rain. Pulling aside the curtain, I watched him meandering down the road. I looked down at my book. Mr. Bacon was being needlessly dull, and his opinions were irritating today. I put him down on the foot-stool, put on boots, and went out.

I kept a discreet distance as he wove down the streets of the neighborhood, out to the edge of town where the heather clustered around the side of the cracked asphalt. Andre was far enough ahead of me that he seemed little more than an indistinct blue shape winding its way through the fog. I kept just close enough to see him until he turned off into a maple forest of bronze early-autumn reds. My tracking skills had gone into abeyance since I had left the boy-scouts at the age of twelve so I hoped there would be a path.

There was a foot-trail, barely trampled down and apparently seldom used. As I turned down it I was almost immediately surrounded by an unseasonable darkness. The trees overhead dripped like limestone rocks. Somehow it seemed that all the wrong animals were lurking. Bats, instead of sparrows seemed to flutter in the trees, and owls were already singing their haunted songs. Raccoons and opossums scuttled across the freshly fallen leaves. In the distance, I could hear a voice like that of a prophet crying out loudly in what I could only assume was ancient Greek.

I was creeping towards it when I heard a great beating in the air, like feathered sails slapping against the wind. Looking up I could see the shadow of something that looked as though it might be an eagle or a pterodactyl, ten feet wide. Immediately casting about for shelter, I found a fallen tree. The giant oak had clenched a great hunk of earth in its roots when it tumbled and now there was a hollow beneath the uprooted base. I hid myself. I could hear the great wings hovering, the terrible beak ready to swoop down and tear at my viscera. I have never been so still in all my life.

Ages of ages passed, then I heard a terrible groaning. I knew that it was Andre, and I also knew that there was nothing that I could possibly do to help him. None the less, Solzhenitsyn had taught me that cowardice is the vice of the slave. I grasped a broken piece of knotted root and emerged.

Andre was bent over a stone altar on which were poured out honey and wine. His clothing, including the fine smoking jacket, were torn, and I could see that he was bleeding. I wanted to take him to the hospital, but what could I possibly say? That Zeus had raped him in the form of an eagle?"

"Andre?"

He looked up. A broken toy soldier desperately asserting his dignity with his eyes. "How dare you...I'll kill you," he choked on his own words. "I'll render you extinct for being here."

"Go on."

"Damn you, Theodorus. Do you know what happens to mortals who look on the affairs of gods? Do you not remember Actaeon?"

"Or Ganymede?" I asked, perhaps cruelly.

"I am going to die," he whined. "You would mock me, when I am going to die. The skies will darken and the rock of heaven split open, Ragnarok will be kindled in the deep, Leviathan rise on the waters --"

I half expected that he would suddenly be transformed into an endangered lizard as a sort of postmodern nod to Ovid, but if reality was waxing mythical today it did not seem to have literary pretensions. He remained before me, appallingly human.

He did not grant me the opportunity to tell him what I thought of his philosophy. The forest had started rumbling, a rustling of sounds like a building wind that I did not notice until it was almost deafening. Through the shadows a horde of living creatures were appearing; not only raccoons and squirrels, dormice and lizards, with their tiny jaws snapping and their petty teeth bared, but also things that ought not have been there: stags and mountain lions, grizzly bears and water buffalo. Pythons, eagles, geckos, moose. A pod of whales. A brontosaurus. Three hippogriffs.

A terrible shrieking and pawing of the ground, a clawing at the air, and a lowing of cattle thundered through the trembling earth. All the battles of Armageddon could not have hoped for such colors, such a dazzling array of uniforms. Pinions flashed, hackles raised, bladders puffed. Impossibly stupid birds inflated giant crimson pin-cushions beneath their bills and warbled out savage cries of war. All the divided kingdoms, orders, genera and species, united as one against a common foe. Crowing, stamping, shrieking, bellowing, her back frothing like a patch-work ocean, nature descended in a fury of tooth and claw.

ACHILLES IN PURPLE

Masculine. A dangerous word because it could mean so many things, and isn't really allowed to mean any of them anymore. Sandra, who is a middle-of-the-road feminist, feels guilty for thinking of her boyfriend Ted as masculine because he likes to watch the fights and is good at fixing appliances. Greta, who has renounced feminism as a self-centered ideology of victimization that undermines the dignity of women, thinks of her husband as masculine because he looks like a Byzantine icon and thunders like an old-testament prophet. Kristine, who has changed her name to Illya in the belief that Troy was secretly a matriarchal paradise to which Helen had fled to escape Menelaus' crypto-homosexual misogynistic energies, is trying to redefine masculinity by dying her male cats pink and naming them "Dawnbeam" and "Young Hag."

Troy: outside the walls, the classical age of Greece. The men are beautiful in motion, sculpted in a profusion of dynamic curves. The women are ponderous geometric constructs, breasts an inelegant intrusion in an otherwise linear form. Helen would not be beautiful to modern eyes. Masculinity reigns. Achilles stands weeping over the body of Patroclus, and there is no one standing by to accuse him of effeminacy. The Golden Age of Man. Masculinity whole and unthreatened. Or do we already hear Plato pontificating in the background, the waves of the Republic rising up the Trojan beach to wash away Achilles' tears?

Kristine nods as though she agrees with this, but one has the impression that she has not been listening. "It's so typical of Plato: all that oceanic grief chained in the dungeon of his subconscious being by an anti-corporeal philosophy. The repression of the feminine Socrates, the Sophia principle, which can only be glimpsed sidewise through the murky darkness of the Platonic cave." She takes a sip her vanilla rooibos energizing herbal tea and smiles like a chesire cat.

"Socrates was a man," Greta points out. "A particularly masculine one, at that, who suffered from an excess of abstraction and a lack of anything that might be considered 'feminine' wisdom. Unless, of course, you want to join the school that imagines anything Socrates said that they don't like was just an accretion put into his mouth by Plato."

"Wasn't there some famous essayist who said that Homer was really a woman?" Sandra suggests tentatively.

"You know, the Homeric mythos is such an androcentric construct that it really obscures the true Trojan womynspirit. So much gory phalo-glorification. If it weren't that Homer had called on the gentle feminine genius of the muse, we would probably never have been able to realize the real strength that proceeds from Helen and Calypso," Kristine rhapsodizes.

"The Nymph," says Greta, "is archetypally a villainess — even if every Sex and the City clone tries to pass off neurotic juvenile self-indulgence as a model of heroism."

After a second of silence Sandra says, "Aren't we supposed to be talking about masculinity?"

"What would we have to say? We're all women. How could we start to define them, if we can't even define ourselves."

"I don't see why we need to define anything at all. The real world is one of non-delineation where male and female are as darkness and light and therefore one."

"Discrimination is the first act of God. Light from darkness. Day from night. Water from earth. Male from female. It's become a dirty word nowadays, but without discrimination, all is without form and void."

"Kind of like nirvana?"

"More like Jean-Paul Sartre."

"The ocean of the absolute where all dissolves in the flicker of Brahma's eye."

"Zues asleep while all dissolves to chaos."

"That wasn't in the movie..."

"The true Iliad is a story of love, transcending gender, transcending rank, transcending monogamy, with the heart of Achilles aching at its center. His love for Briseis. His love for Patroclus."

"And Hector, with his wife and family, slain and dragged around the walls of Troy? One is forced to wonder whether it isn't happening all over again."

High on Mount Olympus, Greta conspires to lull old Zeus to sleep so that the Greek ships will not be burned. Homer does not know her reasons for protecting them. He does not see Aristotle in the future. He has never heard of Thomas Aquinas. On the battlefield below, Sandra stands in defiance of her father's divine decree, her famous shield raised to deflect spears and arrows from the flesh of her beloved Greeks. Her love for them is half-guilty, a sort of self-betrayal, but she can't help loving their shining ranks of bronze helmets, their muscles rippling in the Trojan sun. Kristine, opposite, with a wounded hand and a golden apple, does not realize that the beloved son she has protected will flee the burning Troy only to become grandsire to the Roman Empire, with its male Legions, its male Emperors, its male senate and citizens, and its bastard infants exposed on the roadside.

When Troy lies in ruins, it is Sandra who emerges victorious: she is Odysseus' patron, and she is craftier than she looks.

"Motherhood," Kristine, with her empty womb, says lovingly, "is such a beautiful expression of the feminine self, the life-giving matrix of all creation."

"Are you pro-abortion?" Greta asks pointedly.

"I believe that all women have the right to choose whether and when to share their bodies with another spirit..."

"Mmm. Now isn't that always how goddess worship turns out..."

"What are you talking about?"

"Did you know the Aztec Earth-Mother demanded that one in every four of her beloved children be sacrificed to her in ritual murder? They used to have wars by exchanging prisoners and sprinkling red flower-petals on the battlefield to symbolize blood — no actual fighting. No phalo-glorifying gore. A nice civilized exchange between civilized people. And then they'd strip the prisoners of their weapons and cart them home to be slaughtered on the altar instead. A very feminine form of violence."

There is a long period of brittle silence. At last Sandra says, "This is such a touchy subject. Can't we talk about something else?"

Sandra isn't sure how she got stuck in the middle of all of this. Somewhere, back at home, she was her own woman, she felt powerful and secure, and then the fighting started. She's not really sure how it is that she was taken prisoner, how she became a slave, and she is ashamed one morning when she wakes up and realizes that she has fallen in love with her master. There he lies sleeping, Achilles without his amour, his feet protruding from under the covers. She walks over and leans down to kiss his heel. She hasn't heard Agamemnon's footsteps marching towards the tent.

Looking down from the walls over the battlefield, Kristine can see that something is going on in the Greek camp. She never meant to start this war — all she wanted was to be free, to run away and float like a feather on the breeze, and Paris was so beautiful, with his long hair and his slender features. It has never occurred to her that her lover is a coward. Even now her heart can't accept that all this dying is for her.

It is because of this that Greta hates her. She clutches Astayanax to her breast and prays for her husband's safe return, but in her heart she already knows that Hector will not come back at the end of the war. She looks up towards the heavens, where the music of the spheres sounds silently amidst the eternal perambulations of the gods, and then down, to where the men of Troy are dancing out to meet their predetermined deaths.

"We were talking about masculinity. What makes a man 'masculine'. You claim that there's some sort of deep and significant difference between the sexes, but what is it? I mean, apart from the obvious biological attractions of the other half of the species..."

Greta toys with a piece of sushi and stares out the window. What she said of Socrates is true of her as well: an excess of abstraction, a lack of feminine wisdom.

"At the fountain of our being," says Kristine, "I really believe that we're all the same. We're all fundamentally androgynous."

"Sidestepping the problem," the gears of Greta's mind are turning, like Neptune rolling into Aquarius. "An androgyne is a combination of two principles: of the masculine 'andro' and the feminine 'gyne.' It doesn't get rid of masculinity and femininity. It just muddies the waters."

"No one doubts that there is a feminine principle. A loving, nurturing, healing, life-giving energy that pervades all things --"

"You're doing the opposite of what you accuse the patriarchal establishment of having done. You're taking all the good parts of human nature and lumping them together as 'feminine.' Leaving the dung heap to the men."

"Maybe," Sandra rallies her courage, "maybe it's something too simple to be broken down. Like the color red. Everyone who can see, can see that its different from blue. But you can't really tell a blind person how its different. You just know that it is."

Achilles is dead, but Odysseus has not forgotten how to weep for the fallen hero.

Kristine never met the demi-god with the fatal heel, and in ten years she never learned who Odysseus was either. He never became anything more to her than a plaything in her mind, an amusement that she mistook for love. Now that he is gone she sits weaving alone on the shores of an island, looking out to sea. Neptune has quelled his fury. She looks into the waves where her lover has gone, and she sees her own reflection.

A world and a hundred adventures away, Greta sits before a different loom, unwinding the threads that she spun the day before. She has been waiting for Odysseus for twenty years, and now that her son Telemachus has boarded a ship and sailed out to find him, she too is lonely and frightened. The endless process of weaving and unweaving, constructing and tearing down, has taken its toll on her fingers. She knows what she is waiting for, and in twenty years she has not forgotten his face. She hates the new men, the mewling, self-important infants clamoring for her hand. But she is starting to lose hope, and she doesn't recognize the aged, rag-clad stranger waiting in the hall below.

It is Sandra who brings the stranger up and bathes him. She rolls back his rags and she sees the old scar — not a battle wound, received in all the far-off campaigns of Troy, but a childhood injury. Something that he carried out with him from the beginning. She too is old, now, and she recognizes the boy that she once nursed. With a stab of grief and joy she realizes that she had given up on him. Had begun to weigh in the silence of her heart the faces and bodies of the suitors thronging in the hall below. She had not really expected him to return.

THE DYING PLACE

The lights went down over Fairfield, and at last we were alone. Autumn mist hung around her ankles, and I could see the faint twinkling of light kindling in her hair, that elusive luminescence that was only visible in the darkness. She turned and looked up at the stars, "Make a wish," she told me.

I closed my eyes and wished silently, blowing out the intention between my lips. The seeds of an invisible dandelion scattered in the night air and I looked at her, and smiled.

"Fool," she said. "You should have made a wish that could come true."

My hand reached towards hers, automatically, but she pulled away. She had more sense than I did. "I thought one ought to try to believe six impossible things before lunch."

"This is well after lunch." She sat down on the grass. Dew sprung up beneath her, as naturally as mushrooms spring up after the rain. When she was gone, I would gather up some of that dew in a handkerchief, and I would tuck it in under my shirt to comfort me throughout the day. It was one of my little rituals, which of course she knew nothing about.

I sat down beside her. The grass was cold through the seat of my pants, but she emitted a strange warmth that kept the evening chill at bay. "You know," I said, "that you're the only girl I've ever loved."

She smiled. There was never any sadness in her smiles. She was, I think, immune to sadness. Sorrow, certainly, and a kind of intense compassion that could break your heart, but never anything simple like sadness. She left all of that to me. "I think," she said, "that we had better talk about something else."

Sigh. The great irony of my life. After I had finally given up completely on the hope of ever being straight, I had fallen in love with a woman. Or something like a woman at least. And now it was only a matter of days, at best, and her work would be done and she would be gone.

Morning brought with it a scent of wet cedars, and a sharp blast of reality. The little cabin where I had been sleeping had a woodstove in it, but by the time I had dragged myself away from her company and put myself to bed I had been too tired to build a fire. The blankets were therefore cold, the floorboards icy, and the prospect of getting out of bed weighed on me like the shadow of the rock must have weighed on Sysiphus.

After a long time I managed to drag myself out into the cold air. I dressed warmly and made my way up the house where muesli, pancakes and fair-trade coffee were being served. The house, at least, had central heating. The walls were decorated with improbable scenes of old women giving up their spirits to the earth, happy spectres leaning down to kiss their bodies goodbye, free beings of pure energy wafting across the heavens lulled by the music of the spheres. I thought them rather horrid.

"How was he last night?" I asked my host. She was a woman with long grey hair only recently released from a braid. Her hands reminded me of a van Gogh sky, the skin arranged in improbable swirls with creases where any number of mysteries might hide.

"Very well," she said in a slightly syrupy tone of voice. "I think he's very close to ready now."

I swallowed hard. Grief was not supposed to happen here. Grief, according to the pamphlets, was the product of a cultural prejudice against death. The patriarchal desire to dominate nature translated into a state of war between man and his necessary end. I suppose that Sean believed in all of that, which was why he had come here. To me, it seemed as shallow and unconvincing as the pictures on the walls.

"Can I go down and see him?"

She looked up at the wooden clock on the wall. "I think the morning ablutions will be finished soon. Why don't you sit down, enjoy your breakfast? You need to remember to take care of yourself."

Sean was sitting up in bed. He was awfully thin, and no amount of ritual washing had diminished the sores that were visible above the neck of his pale linen shirt. Before, when we had still been at home, he had been trembling and crying for morphine in near constant pain. Something had changed here leaving a sort of mystic distance in his eyes. I'd been told that this was quite normal, that when the spirit truly reconciled itself to death the body would cease to struggle, and in ceasing to struggle would relinquish its pain.

"Good morning," I said. It was awkward, coming to visit him in this cell. An open coal-fire burned in a basin of stone. The walls were plaster, tinted warm-gold, with a gentle arch towards the ceiling. An oriental pitcher and a tumbler of water sat on a small table next to the teak bed. There were no ornaments, no books, no food. It brought to mind a freshly made tomb, soon to be closed.

He turned towards me an eerie smile. "It is still night," he said softly, "but I can see the dawnbreak looming."

I cleared my throat and perched on the edge of the bed, drumming my fingers awkwardly against my knee. It was, to tell the truth, a long time since we had really been lovers. I'd stayed with him out of a sense of obligation, a stubborn will to prove to my parents that this kind of love could be as enduring as the stars. I'd never really been able to accept it, though, his decision simply to let the illness have its course. It had seemed like I was being abandoned, slowly, for years as day by day he refused to take any medications. Perhaps that was why I wasn't weeping now; I'd already been grieving for the better part of a decade. "Is there anything I can get you?"

"No. I don't need anything now."

"Not even me?" That came out a lot more bitter than I intended.

The smile became condescending. "Don't be like that, Morgan. We've talked about this before."

Yes. About a hundred times. Death is natural, like childbirth. Nothing to fear or to avoid. People cling to life because they don't understand its purpose. They think the road is the destination, the vessel the prize. Bullshit. "I still think it's selfish."

He was silent. It was an argument that I'd only dared to raise on a couple of occasions, because it violently disrupted his equilibrium and made him a bitch to live with for days on end. Now I figured that it didn't matter; I was hardly going to be living with him much longer and he probably didn't have the energy to stew.

"And you don't think it's selfish," he said finally, the beatific grin fading from his face, "to try to make me feel guilty on my deathbed?"

It was my turn to smile. I could feel how twisted and terrible that expression was, but I couldn't keep it at bay. "You're going to a place of infinite peace and beauty, remember? Suffering will be like a fleeting dream. But I'm going to be suffering for a fuck of a long time without you. I just thought that maybe you could descend from your cloud for a moment to acknowledge that."

In the still silence, the distant ringing of a gong could be heard outside. For the moment, at least, the bell tolled for someone else.

"Grief is selfish," he said at last, settling himself back against the padded headboard. "It's sorrow's way of blackmailing joy. You can choose it for yourself, but I refuse to let it in."

"Tonight, I think. If not tonight, then early in the morning." She was sitting cross-legged next to the path that led up to the dying rooms. Since we had come here, nearly a week ago, she had been slowly drawing closer to his cell. The light in her hair was brighter tonight, and there was a sort of emerald glow deep down in her eyes.

"You mean this is it. Tomorrow I lose you both."

She looked at me with the same tender grace that had drawn me towards her in the first place, when I had seen her outside the window of my cabin, on that first terrible night of waiting. "I told you you should have made a wish that could come true."

I was standing up, trying to cut a bold and melancholy figure with my black coat, open, blowing in the breeze. Now a sort of hopelessness settled around my shoulders and I collapsed on the grass beside her. The first pang of real grief formed like a whirlpool in my breast and I realized that everything I'd felt before had only been a prelude. Grasping my own shoulders with cold fingers I bent double and tried without success to sob. My body held on to the pain, unwilling to let it go. "Hold me," I said desperately, reaching out towards her.

She skittered back, out of reach. "You know I can't," she said, "I'm not here for you."

"I don't care," I cried. "I don't want to be alone here. I..." I reached into my pocket and pulled out the old knife with the flip-blade that I carried in case I needed to whittle an afternoon away. I flicked it open desperately, the weird light in her hair reflected on the blade. "Death is natural, after all. Nothing to be afraid of. Nothing to avoid."

"Put it away," she said. "I told you, I'm not here for you."

"Why shouldn't you be? Why shouldn't you just take me too? 'To cease upon the midnight with no pain.'"

"It would be selfish."

"Why is everyone allowed to be selfish except me?"

Her face was cold now, no longer filled with that compassion that had given me hope in the beginning. "Because you know what you're doing. You understand."

"I might understand," I rolled up my sleeve, "but it doesn't mean I care."

The emerald light blazed in her eyes, her hair was like flame, she moved towards me, her white fingers trailing ever so lightly against my face. My body shook under the collision of desire and dread. She leaned back and stared at me. "I wouldn't take you anyways. That's not what I sent for. I would leave you to the scavengers."

I dropped the knife. The sob that had been building up escaped my body, ragged and painful.

"I'm sorry," she said, and I could see that the tenderness had come back to her eyes. "I told you, it's impossible. I wouldn't have a choice."

Grief was building now, naturally, the sobs and the tears releasing themselves in waves.

She stood up suddenly, her body trailing a train of stars. "I have to go now," she said, taking a step towards the cells. She turned, momentarily and blew me a kiss, "I'll see you again, later," she said, "when your time comes."

PEDRO'S TREASURE

Pedro was supposed to be working in the gold mines when the madness took him. They called it the devil's sickness, for how else could one explain a disease that made a good boy doubt everything that he had ever known, and call his own father a liar?

At first they did not know what it was. He had not been at the mines, and no one could say then, or later, where he had been instead, except that he came in at dinner time, and his face was shining with sweat and oil, and he was in a state of great agitation. His old grandfather had just been folding his hands to say prayers over the evening meal when the boy stumbled in through the door of corrugated plastic and seized his sister by the shoulders and cried, in a tone of mystic exultation. "There's nothing there! I've seen it. I've seen it with my own eyes. I looked into the gold mine, and I could see that there was nothing. No gold! All this time, Theresa, all this time, and there has never been any gold!"

His mother took him to bed and felt his head for fever, and his grandmother made a potion that smelled of dead cats and camphor oil and made him drink it, and all the time he continued to say that there was no gold.

When his father came home, with dust under his fingernails, he felt Pedro's head as well, and since there was no fever, he beat the boy soundly on the ear and said, "What is this, then?" and pulled out the money that they had paid him for his work that day. "What is this? You think they pay me for bringing them nothing? For dust? Our village has had gold out of the mine for a hundred years, and it is still not mined out. What sort of stupidity are you spouting?"

"Forgery," the boy gasped. "All a forgery...robbery...lies..." but he said it in a far-away voice, as though he had just seen Christ turn wine to water, and thought it as great a marvel as water into wine.

The best doctors were called in — or at least the best doctors that could be afforded — and a call was put out for a priest to come from a neighbouring village, since there wasn't one in that part of the mountains at that time. It was said that there was a 'specialist' that he could be taken to in the city, but Pedro's grandfather knew better than to trust his grandson to a Yankee witch-doctor full of spells and hypnotism and pills that changed men's minds. When the priest arrived, he said there didn't seem to be a case for exorcism, but he said prayers of deliverance and prescribed a novena to Our Lady of Guadaloupe, and another to St. Dymphna, the patron of nervous disorders.

His mother wept day and night for her son, and his father brought home a nugget of gold as proof, smuggled out of the mine — though he had never stolen in his life and scrupulously returned it the next day. Pedro's sister dragged him into town and showed him the image of the madonna with the golden crown, and asked how it had been afforded if there was nothing in the mine. To everything he said, "Dross," or "Forgeries," and he laughed to himself in the night, a strange, low laugh that, even though it was very quiet, prevented everyone in the house from sleeping.

After that, his father tried to force him to go back to work so that he would see it was real gold they were mining, and his mother knelt beside him and begged and pleaded and shook his shoulders and made great puddles on the edges of his shirt. But nothing was of any use. Beatings he took with the air of a martyr, and to tears he replied with a dreamy, red-eyed look.

It was in the fifth day of his illness that he started bringing home the insects. Not live insects. Dead insect husks, some with icons of devilish saints painted on their exoskeletons, others reddish-brown with long crooked limbs, and others flat and unburnished and black as coal. Peridot, he would call them, or opals, or in the case of some specimens that were not special to any other eyes, rubies. He ranked them according to their preciousness, and the next morning he collected together scraps of old tin and made a shrine where they could be displayed. In the mornings he would go out and stand on the dusty old mule-path where all of the people were shuffling along towards the mines, and he would prophecy against the deceptions that were being worked by the mine owners. He cried that they had bewitched everyone in the village to see gold in tunnels of worthless dirt, and said they were paid with ordinary stones that their eyes perceived as coin. In the afternoons, he went mining in the jungles for his jewels, and came home with a little pouch full of skeletal beetles to arrange on top of his tin-can. These he guarded jealously, and with such ferocity that when the baby came and tried to crush them in his little fists, Pedro didn't have to swat him or scream at him. He just looked at him with his wide, reddened eyes, and the baby sat down and started wailing until mamma came and took him away.

On the ninth day, a man came from the company that owned the mine. He was not the man who usually came — an affable, middle aged man from the city who was too soft around the waist and pinched the young girl's cheeks and gave candy to the babies. The usual man was ill with some sort of city fever, and the man who had come instead was brown and tough as a nut, and he wore a white suit that was stained with dust. Pedro followed the villagers all the way to work that day, preaching against the mine, and when he saw that a man had come from the company, he broke out into such a stream of vituperance that everyone looked at their feet and shuffled into the mouth of the mine and hid there where they could see what would happen.

The man from the company ignored Pedro. He could see that the boy was causing a scandal, so he called for the foreman, and the foreman coaxed the prying eyes away from the edge of the mine shaft, and got everyone to go back to work. Seeing this, Pedro became so enraged that he began to shout threats and to cast around for a weapon. The man from the company ignored him and went over to the shade underneath a palm tree that hadn't been trimmed of its dead branches, and that looked like a wild old man with an unkempt beard. He sat down in its shade, and lit a cigar, and started breathing long lines of tobacco-scented incense into the hot air. Pedro picked up a rock, the sharpest that he could find, and he ran at the man sitting under the palm tree, and beat it as hard as he could into his head.

The man was tough, as I've said, and his skull didn't crack open all in one go. Pedro had to hit him quite a lot of times — no one counted how many, and there was no one around who could do a proper autopsy. But it was a lot, and everybody knew that. They pulled him away before the man had finished dying, and the foreman and some of the men from the mine threw Pedro down in the dust and began to beat him. They might have beaten him to death, except that his grandfather and his father were there, and everyone respected them enough that they didn't have to beg to be able to take the boy back home.

He was very sick then, and one of his eyes was swollen shut, and he couldn't walk properly. Someone said that the company would be sending out the police, and the foreman warned Pedro's family that they had better not let the boy get out of their sight. His sister, Theresa, was put in charge of him. She watched him, and tried to make him eat black-bean soup and to drink the concoctions that grandmother had prescribed for him. When he was not groaning or refusing medicine, Pedro sat and counted his dried up bugs. He counted them and counted them, and sorted them one way, and then another, and nothing Theresa did or said could convince him to stop to sleep or eat.

It was on the last night, before they knew that the police were coming to get him, that Theresa came back from fetching water and found him crouching in the corner and stuffing something into his mouth. She hung the lantern up on the wall and tried to see what he was doing. He turned his back towards her, and she had a lot of trouble getting him pulled around. He opened his mouth to scream and her, and she could see the broken beetle-legs and crushed carapaces sticking out between his teeth. With his fists, he beat her back, but she managed to grab the tin-shrine, and to pour the bugs out all over the floor. She began to stomp on them, one after another, their carapaces cracking and breaking under her sandals. He reached out to try to protect them, but she stamped on his fingers so that he wouldn't be able to stuff any more into his mouth. He screamed and berated her, and told her that he had to hide them in his stomach, because evil men were coming to steal them from him. Since she didn't listen, finally he fell into a kind of torpor, staring off out the door into the darkness. She finished smashing his treasures to dust, then went to fetch a broom.

While she was gone, he sat there looking down at the thin, broken up legs, and the shattered husks, and the little fragments of dried-up jelly that had once been the living inside of the bug. Then he began to cry. He collapsed forward onto the dirt floor, with his fingers digging holes in the woven blanket, and he cried and he cried. At first he cried because he had lost all of his riches, and then he cried for the killing that he had done, and then, last of all, he cried for the tears that his mother had spilled on his shirt. He cried until at last he began to weep golden tears. Then he laid down his head in a puddle of gold. A sour pain was filling his stomach, and it seemed to him as though the walls of the little clap-board house were twinkling with hidden nuggets. Theresa had just come in with a broom and a pan. "Wake me up early," he said quietly. "I have to go to work in the morning." Then he closed his eyes. He was dead before the police ever arrived.

A Very Long Bereavement

The star was born far enough away that there was no chance it would ever be seen by human eyes. A slowly coalescing ball of gas at the heart of a distant nebula. It was just a baby, in star terms, when the girl in Birmingham reached out to it with her mind and captured its celestial affections. A flash like a sunburst. Bonding. All the aching, burning love that ignites the great lights of the universe. But she was gone in a twinkle of star-time and the newborn star cooled, dimmed, grieving. Inconsolable, it wept for a billion years.

THE FAERY CRY

The first time that she saw him, it was by the brook-side, with the sunset going down above the trees, and the smoothed granite rocks slipping in melted-candle layers down into the shimmering darkness of the stream. Nearly within reach, on the far side of the water, stood a man with hair like spun tar strung behind him in the wind, and a figure, clothed in shadows, at his feet. A woman, obscured by rags, with one slender hand reaching up like a beggar on the point of death.

The image was gone in a flicker of a moment; an extinguished candle. Not a footprint dampened the white-antlered lichens that clung to the rocks where she had seen him standing. She waded through the stream's cool waters, and collected a little of the lichen in her hand. Her fingers twisted through it, the slender branches crumbling with a scent like calcified mushrooms or musty bones. Then she turned back on the swiftly setting sun, and returned home, half-convinced that it had been a trick of imagination, or of light.

She was in her fifteenth year, unaware that she was not yet an adult, still strongly immersed in the faery world of children. Of course by the time that she had returned home, to the comfortable monotony of mahogany-colored living rooms and badly tuned pianos, she did not believe that she had seen a thing. The supernatural was either closer than skin, or distant as the quadratic equation. A plaything of the imagination, utterly rejected by reason. It was refuted by the little popsicle-stick craft-show sculptures that hung turning in the breeze, by the sound of a car chugging emphysemically down the highway. Modernity had erased it.

She laid back in the moth-scented hammock on the front porch and watched the dark ghosts of amplified insects fluttering in the streetlight across the road, and fell just far enough asleep that she couldn't be sure whether she heard a voice whispering to her, or just a dream.

There is a voice that calls the young on the threshold of maturity. It may be goblins winding through the glen, heaping platters of quince and dates, and crying, "Come buy, come buy." It may be the faery whisper that the world's more full of weeping than we can understand. Or the nightingale pouring forth his soul abroad. They all sing the same song, in the end: a song of loving death more sweet than life. A call to wander in the wild, away from home. A call to cold water and eternal sleep.

She had thought that it would leave her when she returned home. The voice that had whispered by the wandering brookside, over rock as ancient as the continent, seemed a product of its place. It did not belong amongst piles of homework, or the wide-eyed panting of the television screen.

There comes a time, however, when the country house falls quiet. The parents safely sleep. The clicking of a broken clock on the mantel grinds out the midnight hour. And the young woman supposedly sleeping in the basement sits up, reading Wuthering Heights by the light of a shuddering candle, and hears the fingers tapping at the window. She sees it for a trick. The mind has read too much of ghosts and fiendish longing, and wishes to go and free itself amongst the moors.

She reminded herself that there were no moors to be found outside of her window. The red-orange pallor of a street light. The long, black highways stretching towards town. Not even an old crooked beech tree whose spirit might be testing the nerves of those within. She closed her book, and blew out the candle.

In the darkness, in the silence, she heard the voice more clearly. It was not her own, sounding merely in her head, nor was it some half-remembered dream. Whispering of love, it called her to the woods. She pulled her blankets up over her ears and tried to pretend that she didn't hear.

The moonlight had become so tangled in the branches of the trees that she could not make out the path ahead of her. The way was in blackness, except when she looked up. She could not see where her feet were falling, and only by the crunch of leaves left from last autumn, the swept-bare shuffling of packed dirt, could she tell if she was on the path or off. The woods was one that she knew well. Her childhood fort had been in the tree to the side, the one that had been so bent that you could walk its bark-stripped trunk as though it were a rainbow, and find gold-pots buried in the damp earth at the end. Ahead was the tree like Jacob's ladder that reached up to the heavens, and from whose swaying arms you could see the whole world stretching out below. She should have been able to navigate with confidence, but found that she could not. Fear stretched itself tight in her heart, and finally she could not force herself to go forward even another step.

She lay down, then, not certain why she was doing so. The last of the summer shoots were still poking through the earth, and she could feel the soft, damp foliage, and the dry, aging earth as it sagged beneath her weight. She longed to lie there 'til the worms had found her flesh, until the tree-roots tangled in her ribs, and flowers nodded on her breast. Whomever it was that had called her, she knew that he was here, breathing with the wind through the trees, and murmuring in the distant water running in the brook.

Come away oh human child, to the water and the wild, with the faery hand in hand, for the world's more full of weeping than you can understand. She could not remember, not a second after he had spoken, precisely what he said. It was not in words such as men speak with, but in the voice of a wild and distant world, or else through poetry. She could recall the content. He loved her with a desperate love; the love of John Keats clinging to Fanny's hand when he lay dying of tuberculosis; the love of Heathcliff begging Catherine to haunt him after death. He loved her with all the depth of his being—and yet they were forever separated, kept apart by chains of mortal life. He knew, he said, what dreams would come when she had shuffled off this mortal coil, and he promised a life together, unending, full of the gloom and beauty of the night. A life beyond the severing of the veins.

Night after night, he came to her, and the shadows wound around her waking world. She ate little, eschewed sunlight, dressed in mourning not for another's death, but for her own life. In the cold of winter, she refused to wear a coat, preferring the feel of the biting wind through clothing. Pale, distant, heartsick, she grew, as though she had feasted on goblin fruit and could savor nothing in the living world.

And so it was, one night, in the coldest of January, that she took a pocket-knife and sliced open the screen of her bedroom window, and climbed into the night. The lone streetlight hung ponderously over the worn asphalt and muddied drifts. She walked down the thinly shoveled path, towards the woods.

This time the moonlight was thicker than before, and the tangle of the branches overhead stripped to a host of skeletal arms. The path had been trodden down, and thick snow piled on either side, slippery and dangerous, but easily discerned. She picked her way along it without thought, looking glassily into the distance. He had become so real, so close beside her that she could feel his long coat brushing the backs of her ankles, and could almost see him from the corner of her eye. Not as clear as he had been in that vision, standing beside the brook in the summer. But nearly. And much closer.

She could feel him standing there, his eyes on her as she arrived at the side of the creek and took off her clothes and lay down in the water. The shock of the cold spread like a whip-crack over her skin, but then there was numbness. She laid her head back in the water and let it carry her hair downstream, like a pre-Raphealite Ophelia. It was almost tempting to remain there, still and shivering, until the ice consumed her body and dragged her life away. She could feel his impatience, though: a hunger, almost frightening. The little pocket knife still nestled in her hand. He said nothing, but she could hear him murmuring in the swelling water, could see his writing in the cloud that drifted over the moon. He wanted her to slide the blade out of its sheath, the cold metal to penetrate her ice-numbed skin, and her life to drain out quickly, in a stream of blood.

She lifted her hands up out of the current. Unprotected by the water, she could feel the cold of wind as she opened the knife. The blade did not glint dully in the moonlight. It was completely black. A wedge of shadow against the light. She saw him clearly, now, standing above her on the banks. His eyes were not the loving-black pools that she had pictured in her dreams. They were cold and silver, and his face utterly impenetrable except for a vaguely predatory sneer. A moment of pure despair seized her freezing heart. She gripped the knife and held it over the vein.

A flickering of candlelight. The scent of hot mint tea. A blanket wrapped around shuddering shoulders. The feel of tears streaming down her face. She didn't know how she got back home. The knife was closed, laid on a table near her bed. The blue peacock tea-pot was warm and full. She realized that she must have been back for some time. Trepidly, she turned up her arm, expecting to find bandages and blood. There was no wound. Cold white skin stretched over a too-thin arm. Blood still pumping softly through the veins. She was safe, incomprehensibly. She laid back, wracked with sobs, then finally sat up, and drank a cup of tea, to warm her muscles and still her nerves. When she was quiet, she laid down again and blew out the candle. There, in the darkness, as she slowly drifted towards sleep, she could see the outline of a figure standing in the corner. No longer a lover. Silver-eyed, dispassionate, still. Waiting.

A hundred years he had lain in the water, a hundred years since he himself had come to the stream. It had in those days roared like a torrent, before its tributaries had been stifled, and a wooden bridge had stretched across the frothing wave, looking down on the verdurous windings of endless forest glades. He had come in the autumn, in the season of lost-love's stinging, surrounded by moonlight and the nightingale's song, and with the words of the poets raging in his blood, had thrown himself over the edge.

Five times already he had broken his loneliness, and the wind now sang with the songs of those who had come before. Maidens, foolish as the woodcock when he juts his bobbing head over the shooter's range. Faithless as the pale moon on whose tides ships shiver and are smashed against the rocks. Beloved and betrothed, and yet to him they came, down into the rolling waters, and gave him up their lives.

He had clung to them with fingers of algae, purple-black, had held them fast against his bony breast, had felt, but for a moment, the warmth of living air as their last breaths rested like a kiss on his dead lips. But their warmth had quickly fled, leaving behind nothing save the loathsome damp of ghosts and stone.

Younger he had called them, and younger still, seeking the purest maiden blood of youth, called them soft names in many a mused rhyme, and stolen their hearts before the first spring of earthly love had bloomed. But with this one he had been too quick. The brook had been too shrunken, with no currents to hold her fast, and the too-slow seeping of her life across his bones had been like long-dead lover's cold breath curling through the night. He had longed for something richer: the broken vein, the leaking blood, the taste of metal swirling in the stream, and the heady wine of quick, cold, draining death.

Now the spell was fractured, like the last, gray ice of winter, and the song would echo dimmer in her heart when he tried to call her back.

On a rock beside the stream she sat, with an old book in her hands, and though the light poured through his transient form, and cast him like a shadow on the sky, he ventured out to speak to her again. "That I might leave the world unseen," he quoted, "and with thee fade away into the forest dim..."

She said nothing, her head lowered, as though she hadn't heard him, and he could see the story that she read: Christ in the garden, surrounded by the moonlight. The olive branches singing in the sultry eastern breeze, and Jerusalem beneath him preparing for the feast. Drops of sweat falling like blood from his brow.

"Even he knew," he said, "that 'life is but a walking shadow.' Take up the cross, and lose your life, and eat the flesh, and drink the blood. The extinguished Buddha's candle. The flickering of Brahma's eye. Ragnarök, where the gods themselves are vanquished. 'Death closes all.' It is the last star shimmering on the western horizon. The port for which the tethered trireme groans. In all striving and seeking, all men yield to death."

"'Do not go gentle into that good night'," she said.

"You find Christ beautiful, clothed in suffering, sweating his sorrow out amongst the trees. But what of heaven? Brightness? Glory? Endless day? You know the day ill-suits your soul, my love."

When she said nothing he continued, "Tell, have you not known enough of pain? Not trolled the deeps of human suffering? Not tasted rain and found it to be tears? By the darkest depths of sulfur-breathing hell, I tell you, I cannot bear to be apart. 'I cannot live without my life. I cannot live without my soul!' I would forgive you even that—forgive you abandoning me. But to watch you 'grow pale and specter thin and die'—not the body; the cage of clay, but the spirit housed within it, crumbling to decay. The world was not meant for such beauty. It cannot hold, cannot sustain. It will weather you away, like the sea eroding Venice."

"Don't talk to me," she said, "of love and souls and beauty. You don't love me. You don't deceive me. You have been unmasked." Then she unlaced her boot and dipped her foot into the stream. The water was cold, the ice only just

167

breaking, and swirling snow-flake crystals melted against her ankle until it had grown numb. The stream was wider now, the current stronger, and with all his will he wished to seize and drag her in, but all the tendrils of the stream-bottom were dead, and there was nothing to twine around her taunting foot.

After the point when the mirror cracks, the goblin cry echoes no longer in the glen, the music passes and is heard no more, and for a time it seems the maiden has escaped. He found her looking less and less towards him, growing no longer pale but bright, and the fullness of youth lit her lips and kindled her eyes. No longer could he woo her with hymns of darkness, nor meditations on the torments of the day.

But curses are not lightly lifted, nor faeries turned aside by rational disdain. If she would not come willing, there were other ways to draw her, to darken life with shadow and drown beauty with despair. And so he wove a wreath of darkest algaes, of curling leeches and deep-down gurgling things, and into them he breathed the voice of lamentation, and poured the tears of maidens lured beneath his depths, until the wreathes were given life, and noisome spirits nourished at their breast, and these he whispered off into the night, to torment her with nightmares and sate themselves on fear.

Nightly they came back, dripping with terror like thick, rich oil, or bloated and heavy with rank despair. Now when she came beside him in the last of fading winter, she was no longer bright and lovely, but bare and sear as tundra valleys fading into night. She sat by his side like a black Narcissus, not in love with her own beauty, but in hate. Robbed of sleep, and gloom-entranced in waking, like a lily with a broken stem, she leaned over the stream of life and could not drink.

She came for the last time to the brookside when the first spring lilies pushed their green heads through the muddy soil. New growth sprouted from the up-turned roots of the old dead tree that lay across the brook. It was sunrise, but not rosy: a gray, gasping dawn glimmering dully on the swollen stream. The waters swept hungrily along the banks, churlish eddies tearing up grasses and flinging them careless on the turbid foam.

But though the dark stream clawed at the ground beneath her feet, though it beckoned her to join the branches swept downstream, though it called to her with frothing lips and silver eyes, she would not take a step over the brink, nor dip a finger in the churning wave.

She stood as the sun rose high above the clouds, surrounded by the gloom of a thickening morning mist. At noon she heard her name called from a distant road, her mother's voice as thin and desperate as a crow's. But it faded, and still she stood, glassy-countenanced beneath the heavy sky. In the water, all the world's misfortune swept before her eyes, love extinguished and all living hope dissolved.

Slowly the day dwindled, its light faded away, and night crept in with shadows numberless. Still she stood, motionless, unmoving, until the dark had settled on her shoulders and a wreath of shadows twined about her head. She stood until he rose again before her, gaunt and violent as a late winter storm. And still she stood when his voice solidified around her, black tendrils like seaweed drifting through the air, twisting to ensnare her throat and arms. She stood as the current of his curses dragged her towards the stream, staring down at the turbulent waters darkening in the night. Silent, she stood, but his threatening could not move her, his tugging hate remove her, his curses not reprove her—on the bank, within his grasp, she stood but would not enter, until her toes had put down roots, her ankles sunk and grown into the ground. Deep into his breast she sank her roots, and drained from him the life that he had stolen, stretched her branches out above him, and for a hundred years stared down into the water, silver-barked, returning spite for spite.

It was thus that I met her, as I sat on the stones beside the sparkling water, with the spring leaves slowly blooming into summer. I saw, for an instant, a face reflected—a dark eyed woman standing over a demon's grave; the face of a drowned man shimmering beneath her. The wind in the branches whispered sighingly of love, and a single fruit dangled, silver-downed above me, ripened out of season, sweet to tongue and eye. And I, a human child, by the water, in the wild, heard the faery cry "Come buy," and plucked the fruit, and sucked it dry, with stained mouth and lustrous eye—and now the tree and stream reply, "Seems it not rich, my love, to die?"

LOST VOICES

Dear Dr. Meyer,

I have a curious request to make of you. It is my understanding that you have, in the past, been of help to people with difficulties similar to my own. I would, for example, cite the case (1996) in which you aided a man in the removal of his leg in order to satisfy his sexual predilection for amputated limbs. My case is similar in that it is equally unusual, and equally prone to be misunderstood vis a vis the wider community, and it is similar in that it requires the services of one as deeply committed to patient self-determination as yourself. It is different in that it is a request entirely devoid of sexual implications. If I have misunderstood your motivations and intentions in the case aforementioned I apologize for my presumption.

To make myself plain: I wish to have my vocal chords surgically removed. I require the services of a skilled surgeon who is willing to ask only those questions that are strictly legally and medically necessary in order to confirm my consent to the procedure. I hope that you will be willing to accomodate me in this admittedly bizarre request,

Yours sincerely, etc.

Corina LeClair

She hit the send button, and immediately regretted it. The note sounded artificial, almost archaic, and communicated none of the urgency of the situation. It suggested that her request was the result of a mental aberration, some sort of fetish or private fixation. It communicated nothing.

Still, it was too late. It was already gone.

It was three years, now, since last Corina had spoken. The day on which she had entered into this silence had started ominously enough with a thin drizzle falling on the dew-soaked earth. A text message on her phone had informed her that the picnic she planned to attend that afternoon had been postponed on account of the weather.

For about five minutes she sat in her apartment, listening to the sound of rain on the windows, sipping a cup of tea while she tried to think of something to do that would get her out of the house and out of the rain. She remembered a sign on the highway advertising a tour of some local caves. It was something she'd always intended to check out, and now seemed an ideal time. Picturing a dangerous descent into the depths, she packed herself a back-pack complete with flashlight, extra batteries, dried fruit, jerky, good new rope and a whistle in case she got separated from the group. She drove out of the city and booked herself a tour.

Armed with a map from the kiosk, she followed the tour group down into the darkness.

Or rather, down into the stale electric light.

Long, orange-coloured stalagmites were clearly lit by a series of bare bulbs stretched along a pale-blue cable attached to the side wall of the cave. There was a sound of rushing water underfoot, and every so often a little bit of an underground river could be seen bubbling darkly through a gap in the rocks. The floor, however, was protected by a boardwalk that had been built through the caverns to facilitate wheelchair access. There was beauty here, but certainly no excitement.

As they progressed, the tour guide pointed out several side-passages leading down into the darkness. He explained that most of these were considered dangerous except for expert spelunkers. Some, he said, wound down for miles into the darkness and there were numerous byways that had never been explored. To make up for the disappointment of being unable to explore these caves for themselves, the tourists were provided with a foam display of laminated pictures showing some of the things that had been found deep within the earth.

"It's believed," he said, "that the markings on these walls were made by an ancient peoples who lived in these caves but as you can see, the pictograms are barely visible now." A build-up of pale, yellowish salts had almost entirely covered the wall, and the writing — if it was writing at all — had been reduced to an incoherent pattern distorted by crystal formations.

Corina looked at her map. It gave a basic idea of where the side-channels split off of the main cave, and of which one led down to the room with the ancient writing. Although she was usually cautious, today she had packed for adventure. It irked her to be in a cave full of wonders, yet confined to the one predictable path where the greatest danger was that she might step off the boardwalk and get water in her shoe.

She straggled along at the end of the group, watching for an opportunity to slip away. Half-way through the tour, it came. The guide said that he was going to turn the lights off so that the group would be able to appreciate the darkness of the subterranean environment. The electric buzz of the cables went silent, and blackness enveloped them. Into the blackness, the tour guide spoke of how the caves had appeared when the first explorers had discovered them back in 1867. As the rest of the group were lulled by the recitation of vicarious excitement, Corina silently picked her way back along the boardwalk, around the bend, out of sight.

When the light came back on she was separated from the others. It was not far to the side channel that led down to the cavern of crystals and ancient runes.

The reply that she received from Dr. Meyers was brief:

We will need to meet in person to discuss your needs. Please make an appointment with my secretary.

A phone number was provided.

She stared dumbly at the screen. She reread her own letter. No. She had failed to make it clear that she was not able to discuss the situation except in writing. As quickly as she could, she found the words to write back and explain the problem.

The reply came quickly.

If there is no medical impediment preventing you from speaking, then you are likely to be diagnosed as a psychological case. For legal reasons, I would not be able to proceed under such circumstances. If you are able to bring yourself to have a brief consultation, I would in theory be willing to consider your request.

The doctor, clearly, did not understand. She'd been right. Her first e-mail had been all wrong. It had communicated a kind of stand-offish, dispassionate attitude, as though her desire to be rid of her vocal chords were a just a private eccentricity — like women who wanted plastic surgery so they could look more like cats. It sounded that way because she had stolen those words, lifting the phrases piece by piece, sometimes word by word, from other people's writing that she had found on-line. It was easier to write that way. Less dangerous. You could pretend that you were building a puzzle instead of producing a communication. It was safer, but therefore sterile.

She sat for a moment, staring out of her window over the sea of city lights. A scream was there, rising up in her throat. She forced it back, biting hard on the edge of her hand until the scream had retreated, back down into her chest. When she finally pried the base of her thumb out from between her chattering teeth it was deeply bruised, throbbing, purple. Deep in her throat, the scream was still there.

When they had taken her from the caves, she had spent nearly two weeks in the hospital. She had not spoken a word during her convalescence, and as the days lengthened into weeks and then months her mother had become increasingly desperate. There had been CAT scans, visits to various psychiatrists, even a psychic had been called in to try to pry out the cause of Corina's silence. Corina said nothing, wrote nothing, communicated nothing.

Finally, her mother took her to a hypnotist. She was taken into an office and told to lie down while a needle was prepared. The doctor began to explain what was going to happen: "One little prick...you'll just feel like you're asleep..."

The word "No!" had very nearly burst forth from her lips, but she held it in. Pushing the needle aside, she fled first the office and then the medical building, hiding herself near a dumpster behind the grocery store next door, shaking. Finally, she worked up the courage to make her way to the nearest library and secured access to a computer.

The blank screen stared her down, a threatening emptiness ready to devour words and then cough them back up in stark black and white. It took all of her fortitude just to type out the first letter, "D." Staring at the letter on the screen, trembling with effort, she felt as though she would collapse from exhaustion if she were forced to eke out another. Mapping the keyboard with her eyes, she found the "e," brought her finger so that it was hovering above it, and then, eyes closed, stabbed down. When she opened them the "e" was there on the screen, next to the "D." Again for "a" and then "r."

Slowly, slowly, painstakingly slowly, she had tricked herself into writing a letter, pretending at each step of the way that she was only playing a game, just writing one meaningless isolated symbol after another. Every so often she noticed that they were forming words on the screen and panic seized her. Half an hour in, she had written less than two dozen words. The librarian tapped her on the shoulder.

"Time's up."

Corina looked at her in mute despair. She gestured towards the half-finished document. She had no way of saving it, no way of taking it with her, and it had cost her so much to produce it.

"Do you need a little longer?"

She nodded, tears of gratitude welling up behind her eyes. She tried to blink them away.

"Are you alright, dear? Do you need me to call someone for you?"

Head shake. No.

"Okay," the librarian's face was kindly, even though she had a frightening mane of spikey hair. "You take as long as you need. I'll put this gentleman on number 4."

It took nearly five minutes just to calm down enough to put another letter onto the page. Eventually, after nearly two hours of struggle, she had produced a simple document: a plea explaining that she was an adult, that she was capable of making medical decisions, that she was choosing not to speak for private, personal reasons, that she did not want to be subjected to hypnosis against her will. The library printer purred gently and the letter slid into the tray. Her words, set out in black and white. It was terrifying, but not nearly as frightening as the prospect of having other words, unchosen words, forced out of her body while she lay drugged on a couch.

She photocopied the letter several times, dropped one copy off with the psychiatrist's secretary and went home. By the end of the week, she had been declared capable of choosing and refusing medical treatment for herself.

She arrived early in the morning at Dr. Meyer's office. His secretary seemed surprised to see her standing at the door. "I'm sorry, do you have an appointment?"

Corina shook her head.

"Well, I'm afraid the doctor only sees patients by appointment. You'll have to call me after nine o'clock..."

Corina handed her a letter. She had taken the time to type it out in her own words. It read, simply, "I need an appointment, but I cannot speak."

"I see. In that case, why don't you come inside and we'll set you up a date."

The interior of the office was cramped and cluttered. A goldfish swimming around in a slightly dingy aquarium was the only ornament. There was no waiting room, just a couple of old chairs pushed up against one wall in front of a glass pane with a desk on the other side.

"The doctor does most of his work in the OR," the secretary explained, "he really only uses this space for consultations. Now, let me see when he can fit you in. Would Tuesday be acceptable? Say, 11 am?"

Corina nodded. An appointment card was filled out and handed to her. Another hurdle had been overcome.

The passage had turned out to be a snaking, forking formation carved deep into the limestone by ancient rivers. In some place you could hear the roaring of water on the other side of the stone walls but the underground waterway had long ago shifted its course; these passages had been dry for millenia.

The cave wound through forests of stalagmites and stalactites built up like layers of multi-coloured candle-wax. Dark mildews and slick bacterial blooms stained the surface of the stone, and crystaline structures grew in the gaps where some geological calamity had long ago rent the rock.

Corina had a notepad with her, and took careful notes as she went. At intervals she left markers for herself, a trail of objects dropped from her purse. An old case for contact lenses. Several buttons from a sewing kit. A tube of used-up liptstick. Things that she would not be sad to lose, though she had every intention of reclaiming them so that they would not be left to litter the floor of the cave.

For hours, she wended her way along in this manner, often finding that the passages had curved around on themselves. At first she avoided tight passages and squeezes, remembering how easily rocks could collapse on an unwary climber, but after its initial attractions had been exhausted there was a kind of curious monotony about the environment, twinned with the promise that at any moment she would glimpse a miracle in stone unseen by human eyes since the earliest days of world. Her caution diminished and she started to pull herself up into small gaps, crawling on her hands and knees, trying to find the cave with the ancient writing.

In the darkness, the forms that she had seen in the picture had started to take a hold over her mind. Now she could see them in her imagination, clearer, she was sure, than in the picture itself. It seemed increasingly that the photograph had been badly taken, that it would hardly be difficult to reconstruct the ancient symbols if one were actually standing there, looking at the wall rather than looking at indistinct markings obscured by a camera flash reflected off of crystalline shards.

The strength of her flashlight dimmed until it was only a small, orangish halo on the wall in front of her. She replaced the batteries. Assuming they had been fresh to start with, unless she turned back now she was liable to end her journey depending on the light from her cell-phone.

When she turned the flashlight back on, the beam illuminated walls covered in flaky mineral deposits. They looked so similar to the salts that had covered the writing in the photograph: there was every likelihood that she was in the right part of the caves. She pressed forward into the darkness.

The room opened suddenly before her. It was a broad cavern, and seeing the markings on the wall at this distance there could be no question that they had been deliberately made, that they had meaning. Just barely visible beneath the thick, trickling streams of minerals that had built up over the surface, she had the sense of something terrible, hideous, and yet inexplicably attractive. She moved towards it, exploring it first with the beam of her flashlight and then with her fingers, gently dusting away the crumbling deposits from the surface of the image.

She had continued with this work for hours. The crystals had so deeply abraded the pads of her fingers that they left bloody trails across the wall. Her flashlight battery began again to dim, but she continued working until the last dim glow of the bulb went entirely dark. She switched back, then, to her original batteries and cast the orange light across the cave wall.

There was no describing the image that she had excavated. On the surface, it was mere writing but somehow its meanings had seeped into her fingers as she had touched and caressed and cleaned the black meandering curves of that unknown script. Words began to form themselves inside of her head. They pressed against her throat. Deep, guttural words from a time before history. Words whose terrible import she couldn't explain, even in her own mind. As she began to speak them she was seized with horror, and she began to scream, to scream and to scream in order to try to block the words out.

It was the screams that brought the rescue team to her. Afterwords, they swore that you could hear her all the way up at the mouth of the cave and no one could explain how a human voice could make such a sound. She was unconscious when they found her, but still screaming. Only a deep sedative finally quieted her cries.

At the hospital, later, they told her that she had screamed for so long and so loud that her lungs were literally bleeding from the inside.

"If you had gone on just a little longer," the doctor told her, "you'd have drowned in your own blood."

Her medical records from that day were among the papers that she set down in front of Dr. Meyers when she arrived in his office. Along with them there was a simple note. She had worked on it very hard, for a very long time. It had been produced by hand, written in a series of dots that slowly connected into letters, thickening lines that traced out an odd, meandering script. It read "If I should speak, the world will be ended."

The doctor looked at her for a long time, silently surveying. He glanced again over the statements that had been made by her rescuers when she had been brought in.

"All right," he said. "I'll book you in."

CATALINE

A Page That Will Not Turn

I was lying on the grass next to the swimming pool. In front of me there was an open book. The breeze was sighing gently through its pages, causing them to rise and fall in a slow rhythm, but the wind wasn't strong enough to turn the page. Sunlight coated my back like warm wax, as if it were taking an imprint of my body. My limbs felt heavy, but I wasn't tired.

It must have been a long time that I lay there, because a kind of chill started to creep over me in spite of the sunlight. I forced myself to sit up and realized that a soft, faintly phosphorescent blue moss had grown over my body. It hung in long tendrils from my shoulders and my hips, and its webbed print traipsed across my midriff like fishnet. Looking at my own reflection in the glass doors of the sun-porch, I was impressed by the design. It was daring, provocative, a chic juxtaposition of sharp

189

asymmetrical lines and flowing, organic curves. The neckline rose up almost to my jaw on the right, and then plunged in a risque sweep, just barely concealing my left nipple. The color was perfect. It brought out my eyes and accentuated the blond streaks in my dark hair. Stunning. I spun around for myself a couple of times, making sure that nature hadn't crossed the line between sexy and trashy. She hadn't. Her style was impeccable.

"Mom!" I opened the door to the porch and called into the house. "Mom, come and see this. You'll never believe. It's like the coolest thing ever!"

There wasn't an answer. I figured that maybe she was on the phone, or out front sweeping the walk or something. I walked back over the poolside and trailed one of my feet in the water. I wondered idly what it was I had been reading. I didn't remember reading anything. I picked up the book and flipped it open to the first page. A pencil fell out and thrust itself, point-first, into the lawn.

"October 7," the book said, "Dear Diary." I knew that I wasn't supposed to read other people's diaries. Not that I knew anyone whose diary I would want to read.

`No. I wracked my brain. Not that I knew anyone. Even Mom was just a word that referred to a kind of person that I lived with. I couldn't remember her name, for example, or what she looked like.

Weird. I flipped past the actual content of the diary entry, which seemed to be mostly boring and about boys, to see if the person had signed off. There was a signature. A beautiful, calligraphic "C" followed by an exquisite and totally illegible scrawl. Then an "O," with a Victorian flourish, and what might have been an apostrophe-H, followed by another scrawl.

On a whim, I picked up the pencil. I let my hand gracefully, easily trace out the same name. I was surprised by how easily the curves flowed from my hand, as though I'd written it a hundred times. But that was silly. This wasn't my diary. My name was

My name was

I dropped the pencil. I couldn't remember my own name. Panic started to waken inside me, a coiled snake rising out of my gut. Automatically my hand went for a non-existent pocket and tried to fish out a bottle of non-existent anxiety pills. It closed on a handful of moss that left an iridescent blue stain on the palm of my hand. "Mom!" this time I shouted in earnest. I ran towards the house and pulled open the door. "Mom!" I could hear myself screaming as the panic sank its fangs into my throat. "Mom! Mom! Mom!! Dad!!!!" I realized that my fists were beating against the door of the house. Why wasn't I just opening it? Oh. Because I had tried that. Because it wasn't opening. Because it was locked.

I slumped down inside the porch and pushed hard against my gut, as if I could drive the panic out by pure pressure. I hated myself being this way. Like a baby. "Shh," I whispered. "Calm down. Calm down." Only then I went to say my name, and remembered that I didn't know it, and the panic struck again constricting my throat until I felt like I couldn't breathe.

"The diary," I gasped to myself. "I must have amnesia or something. The diary will help me remember. Okay?"

Panic subsided but I could still feel it there, swaying in my windpipe, a charmed cobra. I went back outside and picked up the diary. "Start at the end," I told myself. "Start with the most recent things."

A Train of Mornings After

"Ticket, please."

I looked up from my seat. The world outside of the train window was passing by in a blur, now suggestive of countryside, now of those little cottage-villages that you find outside of German cities. I tore out a page from the diary and absently handed it to the ticket-taker.

"Ah," he said. "Well, Fraulein, this is your stop." He picked up my valise and gestured towards the door. I made a slight curtsey, feeling very much a young lady as I stepped down onto the platform.

I was in my bedroom, with a boy that I had never seen before. His name, apparently, was Trevor and he was standing in the window, letting the light fall across his chest as he smoked a cigarette. I had popped the screen out so that he would be able to smoke without the smell of it filling the room. I sat behind him, watching the way that he rested his hand on his hips, the way that those tight, dark jeans wrapped themselves around his ass, the slight suggestion of underwear just visible above the waist-line.

"In the movies," I said, "men always smoke after."

He shrugged and tried to look cool like he'd done this a hundred times before. "Some men do it one way, some do it another way."

I could tell by the way that he took his pants off that he hadn't done this a hundred times before. Maybe not even twice. We made out for a while beneath the twined bars of my headboard, which formed themselves into a heart-shaped knot. He played with my body, his hands sweaty against my skin. After a while he fumbled with my fly-button. I slipped off my pants to save him the embarrassment.

He was inside of me for less than thirty seconds when he came. I grabbed his hips. Strange, how I'd never noticed that they were bony beneath those jeans. Wildly, as if seized by passion, I brought his body into collision with mine. Again. Again. Again. I tried moaning, as if the trembling of sound through my body would cue a response. It was hopeless. Like when your coffee has gotten too cold, and you can't dissolve the sugar no matter how long you stir. I closed my eyes and faked it.

He rolled over on the bed beside me. "So?" his body asked me in the awkward silence.

"You were fantastic," I replied. "Divine." I watched his ego swell. Already, in my mind, I was condemning him to rubbish heaps of memory. A rough draft of a letter that I would never send.

I smoothed my hair, readied my passport, climbed back on the train. "I'm sorry," I said. "Wrong ticket," and handed the ticket-taker another page.

He was cute. I'd always found German boys cute. Not Nazi types, but shy young men named Hans who have that air about them of knowing they're boys, but also knowing that they are expected to become men. He consulted the paper.

"I'm sorry, Fraulein. There seems to have been a mistake. This ticket is for the same station."

With as much aplomb as I could manage, I retrieved my ticket and scanned it. There were differences. The boy's name was Martin, for example, and he didn't smoke, and I had a pet turtle that Martin pretended to be interested in before we had sex. Next page, similar. Next, the same. I sat down. I could feel a fierce blush spreading down the back of my neck. Did the German boy know what it meant that all of my tickets came to the same destination? "I'm not like that," I said with a kind of desperation that only made the situation worse. I fumbled through a few more pages, and finally managed to find one that talked about something else. "Here," I offered it to him with a thin smile. "This is the one I meant to give you."

He looked as if he were carefully keeping his private opinions private. "Yes," he said. "Everything is in order."

There was a chime, and a voice saying something in German — probably that the doors were about to close. The ticket-taker moved on to the next car.

I buried my face in my hands. I was a slut. And a ditz. Only, I wasn't. I wasn't like that at all. I was deep. I had thoughts. I could use words like "juxtapose" and "necropolis" in a sentence.

Something had gone wrong. Something had gone terribly wrong. The fragments of myself that I held in my hands, they were not really me.

After a while, I scanned them again, those incriminating pages. There were some weird things about them. Like at the end of one, I had written "Soooo disappointing. Can't wait to forget! :)" and on another, "This time was just bad. I wonder. Is it always like that?" I vaguely recalled that there's some condition people get where their memory is totally shot and they can't recall more than a couple of hours at a time. Maybe that's what I had. Maybe it wasn't that I was stupid or shallow. Maybe it was just that there was no point in being responsible if you could never remember the consequences of your actions. Only that didn't really explain why I had stopped being so blithely indifferent.

The train pulled up to the next station. Numbly, I stood. I didn't even look at my ticket to see if this was where I was supposed to be getting off.

It wasn't until the tinted windows of the passenger cars were whizzing past me on the platform that it occurred to me to wonder how I had gotten from my parents' poolside onto a German train.

Empty Cicadas

The platform didn't match the train. The train had been sleek, well-engineered, with crisp LED signs. It had smelled like efficiency. The platform was wooden, made of uneven boards that didn't quite line up at the end. There was a small ticket booth with a grimy window and no attendant. A sign hanging on chain near the end of the platform read "The Black Forest." A cobblestone lane ran into the woods.

I perched myself on one of the weathered benches and decided to wait for the next train. There was no one else here, and apart from the lane there really wasn't any way to go. Several flies buzzed around my leg as they circled one another, performing a kind of courtship dance I guessed. After a while I lay down, curled up on the bench, my moss skirt trailing down over my thighs, and fell asleep.

In my dream, I was at a train station. The train so wasn't coming. I looked at my wrist. Shit. I hadn't put on a watch this morning, because I just had to wear these earrings and I didn't own a watch that even half-way matched. The clock above the platform read 1:26 no matter when you looked at it. So time just passed, slow, slow, slow. I drummed on my knee and scanned the platform for hot boys. There was only one, but he didn't count. He'd been in my class back in middle school and the Biggest. Dweeb. Ever. Weird, how much puberty could change a guy. But he still had his nose in a book and he was wearing a worn out t-shirt from some heavy metal band that went out of style in the '80s. Not worn out in a cool, hipster way. More "This was in my drawer, and I didn't look at it before putting it on this morning." Still, nice ass.

I woke up. My moss skirt had grown in my sleep so that now it came down to mid-thigh. The platform had aged as well. There were vines growing up over the brickwork of the ticket office, and weeds poking their heads through the wooden slats. Even the track was overgrown.

Okay, so the train wasn't coming. Probably this was just a dream. Only I had just woken up from a dream. A hideously banal dream, yes, but I could tell that it had been a dream. The clock had looked a bit different every time I checked it, and the t-shirt sometimes had a wizard on it, and sometimes a big skeleton with a scythe and metal eyes. I'd been able to see the boy's face even though I was at the wrong angle. Things like that. Here, everything acted like it was real. My body took up space and moved through it in the right way. Objects were solid. It had the logic of a dream, but not the physics.

Panic, again. I ransacked my purse and this time I managed to find my pill bottle. I popped one out. It nestled in my hand, pure, white, pretty. Hard to swallow without water, but I managed it. Just taking it started to calm me down even before there was any reasonable possibility that the chemicals in the pill had actually started to take effect. I waited until I was sure it was working, and then stood up. I was going to have to go into the forest.

The path was well-tended, the tree branches trimmed so that they didn't tear at my face or claw my legs. I still felt like there were things in the woods, a hundred thousand million places where something could be hiding. I pulled my keys out of my purse and carefully arranged them between my fingers so that they stuck out of my fist like claws. Now I was girl-Wolverine and just something dare try to come near me. The unseen things in the shadows shrunk back and I sauntered past them, swaying my hips as a warning.

I walked for a long time. Shadows shifted, and the leaves whispered overhead. In the distance, I could hear things calling to one another from the tree-tops. They sounded loud and perhaps amused by my performance. My meds were starting to wear off. I pulled the pill bottle out of my purse and twisted it open. But before I poured another tablet into my hand, I had a thought that caused the panic in my stomach to tighten and smile. I held the bottle up so that the light shone through the amber-colored plastic. I swirled the pills around, counting. Ten. I had ten doses left, and no idea how much longer this was going to go on for. All I knew for sure was that I hadn't seen anything that looked like a pharmacy where I could renew my prescription. I recapped the bottle and stowed it in my purse, trying not to think about how the path might go on forever and ever, and how it might never arrive at anywhere, and how I didn't know which of the mushrooms were edible and which ones would kill me, and I didn't even have a lighter on me because I was only a social smoker, and it was getting chilly with nothing on but a skimpy smattering of moss, and --

I stopped. Something was in the tree in front of me. It looked like a girl clinging to the side of the bark, frozen in the process of climbing up the tree. I took a step towards it. It was only the shape of a girl preserved as if in resin. No, not resin. It was flimsy, the color of dark maple syrup, slightly brittle with stretchy white sections wherever the limbs were jointed. A carapace. Like the ones that cicadas left behind when they crawled out of their skins and put on their adult forms. I pulled my hand back. The insect girl was holding on to the tree for dear life, as if she was terrified of her own transformation. The features were familiar: a pointed chin, perfect cheek-bones, upper lip pulled up a little too high as if the nose were trying to reel it in on a fishing line. It was my face.

The sight of it made me feel as though I was clothed in the skin of a cockroach. A faint buzzing filled my ears, and every one of my own motions suggested the clicking of insects joints scuttling beneath the front porch. I felt sick, but certain that if I threw up it would be a stream of amber jelly of the kind that squishes out between your toes if you accidentally step on a junebug.

I picked up a stick from the forest floor and began to violently demolish the husk. It cracked easily, but there was a kind of tenacious membrane that held it to the tree and I couldn't quite scrape the last remnants of it clear. Finally, I stabbed the stick into the ground and forced myself to become centered. It was just a husk. It wasn't me. It didn't pose a threat.

When I had calmed down I returned to the path, took a deep breath, and continued walking. I raised my eyes. Above me, in the forest branches, there were hundreds of human carapaces. Each one bore my face. Some were like the first one, clinging to the trees as if in terror. Others hung down from the branches like children in a playground. Several were stretched out languidly along the limbs, while others had adopted provocative poses and smiled down at me with a hollow caricature of desire.

Tightening my knuckles around my keys and shielding myself with my purse, lowered my gaze and ran.

Candy Apple Smile

I ran until I plunged out into a different kind of forest: an asphalt jungle full of human beings. Living underbrush rustling with conversation.

"Are you alright?" The old man was looking for a reason to touch me. His hand closed around my shoulder, gently, slightly fondling the almost-bare skin. "Your foot, my dear." He pointed. I'd stepped on something while I had been running. I hadn't noticed because of the adrenaline. "Let me help you." His arm slid underneath mine, across my shoulder blades. I lifted my injured foot and hopped, leaving a trail of blood behind me on the pavement.

"You know," I babbled, "I was running from something. I was so scared I didn't even notice leaving the forest."

"Not much of a transition," he said, pointing to where a margin of thick underbrush butted right up against a cracked patch of pavement. "The forest comes right to the edge of the fairground. I guess it'd be quite a shock for someone who didn't know where they were going."

Fairground. That explained the music. Not carnival music, but Country and Western, coming from a bandstand somewhere over to the right. I looked up and saw a Ferris wheel rising up against a blue sky spotted with big, puffy clouds.

"Here we are." 'Here' was a picnic table next to a booth that read "Information." It had a small red cross on a white field fluttering from its pinnacle. A Bristol-board sign read "Ride passes. Balloon tickets. First Aid. " A fat, cow-looking woman came out of the booth and picked up my foot. Her shirt read "Silly Boys Trucks are For Girls."

"Ooo," she said. "That's a nasty one." Then she started to go at the soft, fleshy part of my sole with a cotton ball and some stinging antiseptic. I instinctively pulled my foot away, but her fingers closed around my ankle, holding it vice-tight. "We gotta get it cleaned out," she said. "A little pain now, or a lot of pain later." She was really working down there. I squirmed and bit my lip and tried not to whimper. "There's a bit of something stuck in there. It's pretty deep," a pair of evil looking tweezers were taken from the first-aid kit. I felt them slide in underneath my skin, prodding exposed nerves. I made a screaming, gurgling sound behind clenched teeth. "There," she held up something that looked like a shattered thorn, pleased with her victory. "You wanna keep it?"

I shook my head. As she wrapped a bandage around my foot, the old man thrust something into my hand. It was a candy apple. I remembered that I used to have a tube of lipstick exactly that color, but my little brother had taken it and used it up painting streams of blood coming out of the mouths and ears of all of my stuffed animals. "For a brave girl," he said. "I'n't she a brave girl?"

The first aid woman curtly agreed, and said she had to get back to her booth. There was a child there crying over a skinned elbow. I put my foot up on the picnic bench. At least I was back in civilization. Maybe I would even be able to find somewhere to buy a pair of flip-flops. I craned my head back and slowly licked the candy off of my apple. Did anybody ever actually eat the apple underneath?

The cow-looking woman finished playing nurse, and I stood up and went over to the information booth. "Excuse me," I said. "I kind of got lost in the forest. Could you, like, tell me where I am? Please."

"Well," she said, "you're at the fairgrounds. Over thatta way is the beach. If you go up past the merry-go-round you'll get to the parking lot, and then the highway is just on your left."

"I mean... the name of the town."

She looked blank. "Over thatta way is the beach. The parking lot is just past the merry-go-round. Then there's the highway."

"Do you have a map?"

"A map?" I could see that she was trying real hard to be patient and accommodating. "I guess maybe you could find that kind of thing at Antonio's. He's got a shop on the boardwalk, down by the beach." She pointed thatta way.

"Thanks," I said. I curled my foot to the side and started hobbling in the direction that she had suggested.

I made it as far as the midway before my foot started really hurting and I had to sit down. Blood had seeped through the bandage. I needed to figure out where I could get some shoes.

"I am not going on that thing."

It was just a snatch of conversation. Normal people saying normal things nearby. I wouldn't have paid it any more attention except that it was addressed to a really cute looking boy. Oh my God. The same one from the dream. Only in the dream I had remembered who he was, and now I had no freaking clue.

"We've been on the Ferris wheel five times already. I just want to go on one real ride once." He was talking to a not-very-pretty girl whose colorist had made an awful mess of her highlights. Red, purple and black. Not flattering on that skin-tone.

"By 'real ride' you mean a thinly disguised opportunity to indulge in socially sanctioned masochism."

"I mean something that's actually a ride. Not just a machine that slowly moves you around in a circle for five minutes."

She rolled her eyes, which were possibly her only pretty feature. "Right. So you want to get in a machine that quickly moves you around in a circle until someone loses their lunch and high-velocity vomit gets plastered across your face. Seriously, if you subjected a person's body to those conditions in any other context it would violate the Geneva convention."

"Yeah. We can get into a debate about the subjective dimensions of torture and the moral relevance of consent another time. Right now, I'm going on the Graviton. You can come or you can wait."

He headed off towards the line-up. The girl pouted, tossed her badly streaked hair, then headed off in the opposite direction.

I wanted to wave him down now that he wasn't with his girlfriend, but I didn't know what I would say. "Excuse me. I don't know who I am, or where, or how I got here, but I've seen you in a dream. I don't s'pose you could help?" There was no way. I was dressed in blue moss, and my lips were stained with candy-apple coloring, I didn't have any shoes on, and he had a seriously beautiful jaw. Not happening.

The ride he was lined up for slowed to a stop, and after a few minutes a black door opened in the side of the big, white drum. It swallowed up a group of about twenty people. He was one of them. He was a stranger. No way I was going to wait for him to come out.

My foot was hurting a little less. At least I could walk. On the other side of the midway, there was a stair leading down the side of a moth-grey cliff. At the bottom I could see a beach, a boardwalk, and a line of small shops looking out over the water.

A Juggler of Antiquities

"Hello?" the shop window was turned towards the sea-side. The tourists passing by outside sported parasols and surf-boards. One little girl pressed her nose against the glass before her mother pulled her back into the sidewalk traffic. As soon as she pulled away a kind of sooty film began to creep across the surface of the windows, like frost forming in the winter. I took a cursory look around the shop. It seemed to sell a lot of old bric-abrac: things that looked like they belonged in a posh antique shop next to things that would have been at home in a joke store. Like, for example, a huge tooth in a mason jar full of yellow liquid. The tooth looked like it had been pried from the jaw of a carnivorous elephant or something equally bizarre.

A small bell rested on the counter-top. I picked it up and rang it. The peel was surprisingly loud and low for such a tiny instrument. I quickly replaced it, hoping that it would muffle itself. A rash of strange embarrassment spread across my shoulders.

A marionette of a comical devil bobbed at me from the other side of the counter. Not red with horns; more like the Count from Sesame Street. I stood there for about five minutes, waiting for the proprietor to arrive. The devil seemed to be counting the moments of my hesitation. "One! One minute. Two! Two minutes of waiting. Three! Three wonderful ticks of the clock..." Eventually, since no one else seemed to be coming, I tried talking to the puppet. "I was looking --" I said.

"For me, I suspect." A small door opened at the back of the shop. The man who stepped out was the most incredibly unspecific looking person I have ever seen. It wasn't that he was ugly, or plain, or bland, or even boring. All of those would have been definite qualities that you could have described to someone else. It was more as if every one of his features altered every time that you tried to pin it down. Was that smile friendly? Ironic? Mocking? Warm? Gentle? Even a smile at all?

"For a map. I asked at the tourist booth, but they seemed to think it was a weird thing to ask for. They said that maybe you would have one. Do you?"

"A map?" he stroked his chin. Beard? "Tell me, dear child, what is your name?"

I swallowed. "That's a funny question, actually. I don't know what it is. Except that it starts with a C and and an O...and it has an H maybe."

"Mmmm. I'm not sure I can think of a name like that. Chloe and Charlotte start with a C and an H and have an O. Perhaps you could spell Corah or Conchetta with an H..."

"No, not like that. I mean my first name starts with a C, and my last name with an O, and then I think an H right after."

"Ah. Well in that case the possibilities are endless. Christine. Candice. Cordelia. Cytherea. O'Henry. O'Heany. Ohlke. But you're looking for a map?"

"Yes."

"Of what?"

"Oh. I don't know. Ummm. The city, I guess. Or the...province? If you have one."

"I could sell you a map of the beach."

"That would be okay. I guess."

He reached under his counter and, with a flourish, produced a large sheet of yellowed paper. He flicked a black pencil out of his pocket and went over to the window where, with sweeping, confident lines he traced out the outlines of the world immediately outside of his shop. He drew with incredible rapidity, and within moments there appeared a small boulevard, several trees, some beach umbrellas, and a curve of beach all traced out and labeled with a legend and a compass. The points of the compass he labeled, clockwise, "SRAL."

"Shouldn't that be 'NESW'?" I asked.

"Seaward," he pointed to the S, "Right, Anti-seaward, Left. I've never known my North from my South. Do you know yours?"

"No," I shrugged and did one of those self-deprecating little giggles that I hate in other girls. "I guess not. I'm pretty sure the sun rises in the East."

"Perhaps," he said, "but the shadows are dead-on noon and I haven't seen a clock." He rolled up the map that he had drawn and slipped it inside a long cardboard tube. "Two pounds fifty, please," he said.

"I'm sorry. I don't carry English money."

"I accept any currency. Doubloons. Denarii. Dollars."

I opened my purse and searched for my wallet. It wasn't there. "I'm sorry I seem to have --"

"--A diary. Yes. Several pages taken from a diary." He reached into my bag and withdrew one of the precious leaves of paper. "I would take this."

"It's mine," I snatched it back and stuffed it into my purse. "Besides, that map that you're offering me...it's pretty. I think it's really cool that you draw like that. And I... it's just that I was looking for something a little more..."

"How about a dream?"

"I'm sorry?"

"A dream. I accept payment in dreams. Or rather, in exchange for this I would ask only for a single dream." He pulled back a curtain behind the counter. There was a chaise there of the kind that appears in period dramas about mesmerism. "The map," he said, "is more valuable than it looks." He pulled it out, and unrolled it just a little. I could see that the edges of the map had been growing outward from what he had drawn. "And your dreams are not quite so dear as you may prize them. So how about you lie down for me, and we see if we can't tease a little something out of your head?"

A breeze caused the devilish marionette behind his head to rub its hands together. I couldn't afford to give up any part of myself. I backed towards the door, pulled it open, and fled.

November Beach

Something was haunting me. I was aware of it the moment that I stepped out onto the boardwalk. In the scent of old seaweed and half-dried fish. In the shrill cries of gulls as they circled above the bay. The beach lay below me, a crescent curve of pale sand circling a small inlet of shimmering still water. A concrete bulwark had been set up between the inlet and the sea, and as the waves crashed against it from out there beyond, water gushed through a series of pipes onto the backs of bathers. I wanted to swim but was afraid that the delicate mosses of my dress might wash off in saltwater.

There was a place just down the boardwalk that was selling water-shoes and t-shirts, but I didn't know what kind of currency they took and in any case, I didn't have anything I was willing to trade.

I'd stolen before. Little things that you could easily slip into a purse. Mostly candy, or the kind of jewelry that only costs twenty bucks in the first place. The owner of the stall was sitting right there, watching the bathers down on the beach.

I walked over and started browsing the shirts, waited until he was busy with another customer, and then quietly unhooked a pair of water shoes from the rack. They were on a black plastic hanger, and there was paper shoved up inside of the toes. I pulled out the packaging as quickly as I could and then dropped them quietly to the deck, slipping my feet inside. Pretending to be interested in one of the shirts, I shoved the hanger and the paper into my purse just as he turned towards me. "Do you have one with this design in black?" I asked, perfectly aware that he didn't have any stock except what you could see.

He was probably in his thirties, but trying to look younger. His hair was slicked back with too much gel, and his shirt and jeans were both too tight. Presumably when he sucked in his gut and arranged his fat in the mirror in the morning, he looked good. The moment I spoke to him he abandoned his other customer, who was old and frumpy and looking for a t-shirt for her neice, and stepped towards me, too close. I tried to shuffle back and realized that the shoes were still tied together with a little piece of elastic cord that left me like an inch and a half of room of maneauver. "Whatcha see is whatcha get," he smiled, showing off bleached teeth. "But I think this one would look good on you as is."

"It's white," I pointed out. "And I was kinda hoping to go swimming."

"My lunch break's just about now," he said. "Let me join you, and you can have it for half price." He sidled closer, obviously taking my failure to back away as encouragement.

I giggled awkwardly. "My boyfriend would be jealous," I lied. I gave him my prettiest smile, "You'd better help that other lady. I'll just browse a little more."

His hand whispered against my hip as he turned, reluctantly, towards his till. I fished in my purse for a second and found a pair of nail scissors, bent down, pretended that I had an itchy ankle, snipped the elastic cord. My feet could move now. I was home free. I went to replace the scissors in my purse. The crumpled piece of packing paper from the toes of the shoes escaped as I was putting them in and tumbled, incriminating, onto the boardwalk. I thumbed the shirt rack a little, hoping the breeze would blow it away.

"Hey lady!" a child's footsteps clattered over the boards. "You dropped this." He picked it up and handed it to me, looking proud.

"What's that?" the man with the greasy hair was looking at me now with hungry suspicion.

The frumpy woman looked down at my feet. "I assume," she said, "that you were planning to pay for those shoes?"

Eyes had gathered. Peering, accusing. The shop owner took the crumpled paper from my hand and spread it out. I could see that writing had developed across its surface. A list. Mostly chocolate bars and cheap earrings. His look said 'You should have just agreed to go for that swim.' Silently, he tore the page in half. The list reproduced itself on each side of the sheet. He handed a copy to the frumpy woman, who tore it and handed a copy to the child.

Soon, there were dozens of copies passed from hand to hand along the boardwalk. Slowly, the shop owner began to crumple his into a ball. The onlookers followed suit. I could see that when he opened his hand the wad of paper had transformed into a sharp, pitted ball of stone. He raised his hand.

As the first stone pelted my shoulder from behind, I grabbed the rack of t-shirts and pushed it into the chest of the slimy, shirt-selling man. He fell back, arms circling behind him as he slipped from the edge of the boardwalk down onto the sand. Ducking through the gap in the circle of my accusers, I jumped unto the beach and ran.

They chased me. It was hard to run with the snow-soft sand churning beneath my feet. A cry had been taken up, and I could see that there were more people coming up out of the water to find out what was causing all the fuss. The hateful shoes cushioned my feet against the gravel but I could feel that my foot had torn open where the thorn had been. Stones kept bouncing painfully off my skin. Up ahead, I could see a group of boys who had gotten ahead of me by running along the curve of the boardwalk standing, taking aim, waiting for me to pass.

A surge of adrenaline forced me to go faster. I circled around the boardwalk's end, a hail of pebbles falling on my back. Up ahead there was a cracked, concrete stair leading down an artificial ridge made of blocks of caged rock. A rusted chain swung across it, forbidding entrance, with a metal sign that I didn't have time to read. I slipped under the chain, half running, half-falling down the crumbling steps.

Looking up from the bottom, I could see a few of the people who had chased me, but all of them were standing back from the edge. Nobody was following. As if nobody dared.

The Frozen Stream

The wastes of a stone beach spread out ahead of me, girded on one side by the cracked face of the cliffside, on the other by the silvery waves of the sea. Huge, strange shapes rose up out of the rocks. The nearest must have been half a mile away, but it was enormous: the head of a giant fish. Only the bones remained, huge jaws jutting out of the sand and a half-buried eye socket. I had seen the partial skeleton of a blue whale once, in a museum. This was way bigger. Its fearsome teeth rose like monoliths into the sky.

For a while, I waited, hoping that the mob would forget about me and I would be able to go back up the stairs. Every time I looked up, though, they were still there, watching me like a predator looming over the bolthole of its prey. Eventually, I started to feel hungry. The pain in my foot had subsided. I was afraid of the strange beach, with its harvest of impossible fossils, but I couldn't see any other direction that I could go. I took a pill, steadied myself, and got to my feet.

An old path, cracked like a shattered tooth, wound up towards the cliff. I followed it until it came to a river that flowed down to the sea. A waterfall, thin as angel's wings, cascaded down from the cliffs above. The remnants of a bridge stuck out of the water and I could see that there was a shallow causeway stretching across where the stone of the bridge had long ago tumbled into the stream. The path resumed on the other side.

I stuck my toe in. The water was unfathomably cold, but at least the shoes that I had stolen had good rubber soles, even if they were ugly. I began to pick my way across. It was wide but shallow, with a slippery bottom. The current was strong, sliding between trailing seaweeds along the bottom of the stream.

About halfway across, I saw something in the water. The body of a child. I risked wading out a little into the deeper water until at last I was able to grasp at the edge of her dress and reel her in. Taking her in my arms I lifted her out of the icy water.

The dress. I recognized that dress. We'd been out at the mall, and I'd seen it on a mannequin in one of the shop windows. I couldn't have been older than seven at the time. I'd cried because my father said that I didn't need any more clothes, and besides, it was too expensive. After that, when my mother had calmed me down with an Orange Julius, she and my dad had wandered away to fight. Later that week, the dress had appeared in my closet. It was cream-coloured corduroy with sprays of frosty pink and blue.

Tears sprang into my eyes. This was my first real memory of my childhood. I could even see my mother's face, what it looked like when she held the paper napkin and helped me blow my nose. I held the little body against me, crying in the stream.

Cold. It was as if the chilled blood frozen in the veins of the child had started to seep into my own body. A fatal heaviness came over my limbs and I stumbled, the current pulling at the fronds of moss that clung to my thighs. The weight of the child was like a beam of timber and I fell back, the little body crushing me beneath it, pinning me to the bottom of the stream. I was drowning, but I couldn't let go of that precious fragment of my past.

Something pulled me free.

A gasp. An inrush of air. Terrible bands of freezing pain slicing across my windpipe. I had been dragged out of the water and was sitting by the riverside shivering, the internal furnaces shaking and shuddering with the effort to warm my blood.

"You okay?"

It was the boy. The one from the fair. From my dream.

"How did you get here?"

"The lifeguard. He saw you go down the stairs, but they don't pay them enough to come out here chasing after fools. So he asked for volunteers." He wasn't looking at me. His hands were hooked behind his neck, his elbows jutting out like blinkers on either side of his head. Wet jeans clung to his legs. "Do you, um, need a shirt?"

"Yeah. I'm really cold."

He turned his back and stripped his shirt off. It was one of the ones that I had been so disdainful of in my dream. Faded. Stained. Unfashionable. With an unraveling hem. I put it on. He looked really good without it.

"Thanks," I said. "I noticed you back at the midway. With your girlfriend."

"Sheila? She's, umm. Not really my girlfriend. Uh..." He stared at the rocks for a while. "I should actually get back to her. I promised to take her up in a balloon."

"Oh." I let my teeth chatter a little more obviously. "I'm like, super-cold." I waited for him to take the hint, to offer to put his arms around me to warm me up.

"Right." He clapped his hands together. "Run."

"Run?" I looked around. I couldn't see anything dangerous.

"Run. Cardiovascular exercise. It'll get your circulation going and increase your body temperature. There was one time, I was outside with my brother. We were hunting a wolf, which probably wasn't the brightest idea given that I was nine. Anyway, I slipped and fell into a half-frozen swamp..." he had started running, back towards the cliff face and the boardwalk.

"Stop!" I called after him. "We can't go that way."

He turned around. "Why not?"

Quickly, ashamed, I explained about the shoes.

He looked at me like I was probably an idiot. "You came out here because you were afraid of that?" His eyes cast out over the long, barren wastes, the shadows of ancient monsters. "Just be glad you only got this far."

"But if they're still there…waiting. It's not safe to go back." I pulled his grungy, thread-bare old shirt tight around my shivering body.

"It's only stones," he said. Seeing the fear that kindled in my eyes he added, "If you're really that scared, you can hide behind me."

The May Balloon

"Germanicus, finally. What happened to your shirt?" The girl with the badly streaked hair was waiting at the top of the stairs.

He gestured towards me with obvious embarassement. "She kind of fell in a river. She was cold."

A couple of kids pushed past us, yelling and pointing towards the sky. The cloudscape was studded with hot air balloons, like raisins in a loaf.

"So are we still going ballooning?"

"I have an extra sweater in the car. I'll be right back." He took a few steps, then turned around, remembering. "Oh. Right. Sheila, this is Catty. Catty, Sheila."

Catty? Without even thinking I blurted out, "I hate that name!"

"Sorry. Cataline." He looked uncomfortable for a second, then ran off.

Cataline. Cataline was better than Catty for sure. It was actually kind of a pretty name. It kind of suited me. I pulled out one of my diary pages and looked at the signature. It was a perfect fit.

Sheila asked me a couple of questions to seem polite, mostly about whether I was okay, and how I'd ended up on the forbidden beach. I answered pretty vaguely. I was still kind of embarrassed about how easily we'd made it back. When I'd been alone, my accusers had seemed legion. But actually there'd only been like a dozen still waiting, mostly old people and kids. Everyone else had come up to the cliff-top for the balloons.

Sheila got in line and stopped talking, probably hoping I'd go away. We were close enough now to see the balloons slowly filling with hot air. They were beautiful, with decorative sides stitched up like quilts. The ropes that held them were twined together with garlands of flowers. I could see entire families gathered together in a single basket, little girls strewing flower petals over the edge and singing songs in praise of the month of May. Not really his girlfriend, he had said.

"Do you mind if I join you," I asked when he returned, wearing a polo sweatshirt with red and green stripes that was, if possible, even uglier than the t-shirt. "One of those balloons will totally hold three."

"Uh. Yeah, sure. I guess so."

Sheila looked irked, but smiled politely. The line was pretty short now. Most of the balloons were already off, sailing out over the edge of the cliff. We didn't have to wait long before it was our turn.

Our balloon was decorated with a shepherdess motif: a girl with a wide-brimmed hat and a crook in her hand. We pushed off into herds of puffy wide cloud.

A soft breeze bore us along on her breast, carrying us out over the shining cliffs and the glittering sea. I leaned out and waved to the other leisure-goers who had taken to the skies to enjoy the spring sunshine. The boy, who I guess was called Germanicus, trimmed the flame and the balloon descended towards the water. I hung over the basket-edge like a child leaning over a banister at that critical moment, right before a watchful adult warns them they will fall. The endless ocean stretched out beneath me.

As the balloon sank beneath the clouds, I saw that the sea was full of monsters: tight-packed like bait-fish in a net. Their oily bodies rolled in and out of the water, over one another, flashing fins sharp as razors, tentacles, saw-backed spines. I could see several other balloons that had floated down close to the surface. Tiny figures leaned out of the baskets, readying harpoons. Their smallness gave perspective to the size of the creatures below. The metal barbs shot from the balloon-bows like sewing needles, occasionally pricking the surface of the roiling mass of flesh. The reward, if there was any, was a tiny prick of blood on the water before the harpoon was shaken loose.

Finally, one of the men scored a mighty hit: his miniature weapon went in, caught in the fatty tissue beneath the skin. The monstrous eel began to writhe, its serpent body rising above the surface as it fled over the backs of its companions. The balloon was drawn along behind it, yanked at dangerous speed across the sky. It had descended to the point where the bottom of the basket was skimming along the surface. The sinuous suckers of a giant squid licked across the bow, and for a moment it looked as if the fisherman would be devoured by his prey. He cut the line just in time and the balloon rose back up on the gentle currents of the air, bobbing and rocking, probably with laughter.

"We should so do that!" I exclaimed. It really actually wasn't my kind of thing. Probably I would have a panic attack. But it definitely wasn't Sheila's kind of thing. "Do you think if we went back... I'm sure we could rent a couple of those harpoons. It would be, like, so exhilarating!"

Sheila and I both looked at Germanicus.

"Do you want to?" Sheila asked. It was a barbed question. "I don't mind. If you and Catty want to go out hunting sea-monsters, and get yourselves killed, I can just go and see if there's anything interesting happening at the bandstand."

Germanicus leaned over the edge of the basket. Another harpooner had just caught the tip of a giant octopus' leg and his balloon was being thrashed around in a wide arc as the creature tried to free itself from the painful metal sliver. Germanicus' eyes glittered. "Yeah. Actually, I do want to. Sorry." He closed his eyes, licked the tip of one of his middle finger, and snapped it against his thumb. Sheila wavered for a moment, and then vanished on the breeze. He opened his eyes. A harpoon had appeared in his hand.

"What did you just do?" I demanded. "Where did she go?"

He looked at me weirdly. "Why do you remember that she was even here? You shouldn't. Actually, strictly speaking, there's no reason why I need you either." He snapped his fingers again. I didn't fade into nothingness. He looked surprised.

I repeated my question. "What did you just do?"

He looked away from me with something akin to horror. "Why are you still here?"

I stared him down for a couple of minutes. Finally he said, "You're not real. No way you're real. It's just my mind playing tricks on me."

"What do you mean 'I'm not real'?"

He looked at me with irritation. "I mean," he said slowly, "That all of this is just an illusion. Fantasy. Something that my mind is doing to distract itself from certain unacceptable facts, like the fact that my body is very slowly decomposing – or possibly turning into a soap-mummy – at the bottom of a dark, horrible pit."

"Soap mummy?"

"Yeah. It's kind of cool, actually. Under certain conditions the body won't properly decompose. Instead it undergoes a process of natural preservation and turns into this kind of soapy substance. My particular body is at the bottom of an old sunken well, which could conceivably provide the right kind of anaerobic environment for mummification. Neat, huh?"

I stared at him blankly. "You mean you're dead?"

"Yeah. Dead. You know. Cessation of bodily functions. Cardiac arrest. Termination of brain activity. Dead. I mean, it's possible that strictly speaking I'm not quite dead. I was in the process of slowly starving-slash-dying of exposure when I came here, so maybe my body is in the final stages of

226

mortal agony and my cognitive activity has become completely dissociated from it as a result... I don't know exactly."

I shuddered. It made so, so, so much sense. Waking up beside the pool, not remembering things. But... I didn't want to think about it. I popped some pills, not counting how many. Who cared if I overdosed if I was already dead?

"Anyway," he said, "since you don't seem to be going away, let's go hunt some sea monsters."

Pink Fuzzy Glittery Dice

"I really am real, you know." We were sitting underneath one of the white picnic tents at the fairground eating franks and sauerkraut. Germanicus had a long, shimmering comb that he had cut from the back of a three-headed fish the size of a football stadium. His arms and face were scratched up and he had a deep gash across his chest from trying to slice his trophy free while being slashed at by a fifty foot high dorsal fin.

"What do you think I can make out of this?" He held up the two-foot long segment of sharp bone and tough, leathery fish-skin. "Something Sheila would like."

"I'm real. Re-eal. Like you. I don't remember dying, but that must be what happened. I mean, the

227

way you describe it you must have known it was coming for a long time. I figure for me it must have been quick. Like I dove off the roof and missed the pool, or something."

"No way you're real. You're just a girl that I used to know. Another memory that my mind is using to shield me from the inescapable truth."

"Then why can't you make me just go away?" I demanded.

He shrugged. "I don't know. Maybe because I could never make you go away in real life."

I scowled. "You're not a very nice person, you know."

The insult didn't seem to bother him. "I was a lot nicer when I was alive. When there were actual other people who weren't just shadows and projections of my interior life and they had thoughts, and feelings, and free will, and the things that I said and did mattered. Then I was nice. Or at least I tried to be." He looked faintly guilty.

"I don't remember if I was nice. I don't remember very much about myself at all. Was I? Nice?"

He ate his frank and knocked back his water. "You want a beer?"

Beer is gross. "Sure. Thanks..." So I hadn't been. Maybe that was why I didn't remember things about myself. Maybe you only remembered the good things here and there just wasn't much for me to recall.

He came back with the beer. "All right," he said. "I agree to pretend, for now, that you're real." His smile was really ugly, and not quite a smile. "Maybe that's my subconscious' whole idea. With Sheila I can tell it's not her. She's a caricature of herself. But you were always a caricature, so how will I tell the difference?" He knocked back half of his beer in one go, and then sat staring at it as if it were a source of bitter but expected disappointment. "See? It's the only way to stay sane. I have to find some way to keep believing that maybe I'm not alone."

"At least you remember things. At least you know who you are. I don't even have that."

"I wouldn't worry about it," he said. "There's not much to know. You're a girl. You like shopping. You like dancing. You like boys."

"Just because I'm a girl doesn't mean that I'm some stupid sexist stereotype!"

"No. It doesn't. It's just that those happen to have, in fact, been your only observable interests." He drank the other half of his beer and lit a cigarette. Several nearby patrons coughed, and one woman tapped angrily on a no smoking sign attached to one of the tent-posts. He ignored them as though they were static, background noise. "If there is more to you than that, please, fill me in. I will happily stand corrected."

"I'm not stupid," I said. Only I accidentally inflected like a valley girl.

I could see that he was judging me through a haze of smoke. "It's probably better if you are. Then you can just enjoy the ride, look at the pretty sea-monsters, browse the shops down on the boulevard. I don't have that option. I minored in philosophy, and I'm not able to avoid thinking things through. But if you are real, probably you'll be happier if you just chase after imaginary boys and don't think too much."

I was pretty sure I was starting to hate him. "Yeah? And maybe you'll be happier if you just keep pretending to go out with some girl who wouldn't even date you in real life, and stop boasting about your philosophy degree."

"Minor. My degree's in Classics."

I wanted to kick him. "I was smart, you know. I, like, wrote poetry and read books."

He looked pained. "Look, Catty --"

"Cataline!"

"Cataline, I think this will work better if we just eat our hot-dogs and play some carnival games. Let's not talk about anything that matters."

We finished our food in silence and then walked over to one of the nearby booths. It was one of those games were little forest animals come out of a hole and you have to smack them with a mallet. He was terrible at it.

"Let me try," I said.

I watched and waited, scanning the holes. I didn't wait until I could see movement, just until my intuition shouted That One! Then I would strike. I pounded two hedgehogs, three bunnies and a vole right on the middle of their little rubber heads. The timing was so essential, so important.

"Choose your prize," a bored looking girl with acne scars gestured towards the middle grade of prizes. I chose a pair of glittery dice, the kind that people used as air fresheners in their cars. These ones were pink, with tufts of iridescent fuzz.

"Spin," I hung the dice over my elbow so that each one could spin independently. A peace offering. A twist of fate. Germanicus looked bored but obediently spun one of the dice strings around. I twisted one as well. Once they were both spinning really good I flung them up into the air. "Winner has to give the loser a kiss," I cried as they circled around one another. It was a dumb game that we used to force the boys to play in the schoolyard when I was a kid. The dice tumbled to the ground and both came up fours. I picked up the dice and hung them around his neck, using the cord to pull him in closer. "We match," I said. "That means we both have to kiss each other at exactly the same moment."

He shrugged out from under the dice-yoke and held his hands out in front of him as if he were trying to keep a wild animal at bay. "Look," he said. "That really isn't my kind of game."

"It's fate," I told him. "You and I. We must have died at precisely the same moment, the exact same micro-millisecond. That's why we're both here together, sharing the same afterlife." I felt kind of triumphant: I could think things through too. Only I came to better conclusions than he did. "We may be the only two real people sharing this world. So either we learn to love each other, or we spend the rest of eternity alone."

First Date of Eternity

"So, what do you want to do?" Germanicus was slightly tipsy. His reaction to the idea that he was going to have to learn to love me had been to down another beer.

We were standing at an artificial crossroads set up in the heart of the fair. A stand with bubble-gum coloured signs pointed towards various amusements. The midway. A smash-up derby. A barn dance. The balloons. His boredom was infectious and it was hard to feel excited about any of it.

I paced in a circle to see what could be had in the other two directions. I expected pie eating competitions and beauty pageants for dogs, but instead it offered stuff you never get at rural fairs. Lego world, a film festival, Chinese acrobats. Germanicus reached out and grasped the signpost, spinning it like a wheel. With each rotation came an entirely new set of attractions, the fairground widening around us, the whole world spinning on an axis of desire.

"That's right," his voice was drenched in sarcasm, "you can have anything you want. Except the things that matter.

"You were the one who said we should just go and have some fun."

"Okay." He looked like I'd just set a plate of mouldy cockroaches in front of him. "So choose your fun."

One of the listings was for a place called the club. All the other signs were all caps, but this was lower case, laid back, chill. "Let's go dancing," I grabbed his hand and twirled myself around.

"I don't dance."

"All right then. Choose something *you* like. Anything at all." I spun the sign-post, and a world of possibilities glittered past.

He stopped it, studied the entries. For the first time, a hint of light came to his eyes. "How do you feel about gladitorial combat?"

I stared at him. "Are you serious?"

He shrugged. "Why not? It's not like the people here are real. It's no different from a movie, really, except that it's in ultra hi-def 3D, with five sense surround."

The idea of watching, hearing, smelling and feeling people hack each other to death made my stomach turn, real or not. "I'll make you deal," I said, "I'll do your thing if after you promise to do mine."

"Alright," he shrugged. "Let's go."

Following him was like crossing the threshold into another world. I hadn't really thought about it, but up until now everything had been just like a dream. Specifically, just like one of my dreams. This had come from his mind, and the difference was obvious. Linear shapes, obsessive historical detail. Hard-nosed realism with the colour all washed out. The throngs lined up in the streets all wore ancient clothing, but it wasn't a pageant like the costumes in Cleopatra. Apart from the occasional sweep of red, everyone wore boring shades of leather and linen. And they smelled. A reek of fish and blood and bodies overlaid with some kind of weird exotic spice.

A servile looking man in a tunic met us at the arena door, led us through the crowd up the stairs to a box. The smells were better here: a table laid out with delicacies, incense burning to some bloody minded god. Germanicus had changed his clothes into a toga. It didn't quite suit him, but it was better than that awful sweater.

There was a sound of a gong and a blast of trumpets. From somewhere far away in the pit of the arena a door opened. The scale of it was overwhelming, way bigger than the Colliseum. The size of a battlefield, instead of a stadium. The door was large enough to allow an entire army to march out abreast onto the field. Thousands, maybe tens of thousands of men, accompanied by elephants and dressed in shades of black and brass, dark features covered by their helmets, weilding a forest of sharp, bristling spears.

I imagined myself an evening gown modeled after the shades and shapes of their equipment. A sweep of topaz and onyx across the lids. Dark liner. Wine-colored lipstick. Hair pinned up, severely, in a tight coil so that only an occasional streak of blond would emerge from beneath the black. A gown that could seduce a nation. I looked around for something that I could check my reflection in, but it was weird. In any of my dreams there were always reflective surfaces, even if it was just a pond or a polished spoon. Here, there was nothing. Even the goblets that held our wine were made of ivory, cluttered up with carvings of men chasing maidens and cows with flowers on their horns.

Another trumpet blast, and the opposite door opened. This time I recognized the combatants. Romans. Super-serious guys in skirts. Boring. Dull. I knocked my glass of wine back in one gulp. I normally wouldn't have drunk that way, but it seemed to match my gown. A slave appeared almost immediately and refilled my glass. "I assume you're cheering for Rome?" I said, trying to get his attention.

He was reading what appeared to be a program, written in a language, probably Latin, that I couldn't understand. "Of course. The Romans are being led by Gaius Julius Caesar," he pronounced the name in a weird way, so that it took me a few minutes to realize who he was talking about. "And the Carthaginians, by Hannibal Barca. Two of histories greatest generals, though of course in reality they were separated by over a century and never could have met." He went back to studying a diagram showing the weaknesses in a suit of armour. He didn't even notice my dress.

With a cry the armies fell upon each other. From up here it just looked like chaos, masses of men running into each other, hideous screams and clouds of dust. From the edge of the battle, a man crawled out, clutching at his entrails, so bloodied and trampled that it was impossible to tell which team he was on. I got the slave to lead me off to a back passage where I could throw up.

When I returned, I got my seat moved far enough back that I wouldn't have to see. Germanicus was leaning over the balcony, entranced by the bloodshed and munching on a fig. He didn't seem to be aware that I'd been gone. I was starting to suspect I'd been naive. Until now I had believed the biggest obstacle would be getting *him* to fall in love with *me*.

Whirl Without End

It seemed to take forever, but the battle finally came to an end. Rome had, apparently, won. To me it didn't look like victory, just like heaps of bodies in the moonlight, pouring out bloodied rivers onto crimson-coloured mud. Germanicus was in high spirits, rhapsodizing about various strategies the generals had employed. I pretended enthusiasm for as long as I could, but really I just wanted to get away from the smells of fear and death.

I reminded him of our agreement.

His mood deflated like a pricked balloon. "Oh yeah," he said. "I guess I did promise that." He steadied himself with another glass of wine.

"Come on," I took his hand and led him down the stairs. As we descended, the deep, shuddering breath of a bass drum sounded from below. I painted neon graffiti on the arches and lit it with black light. When we arrived at the entrance to the arena, the stands were emptying onto the field. The soldiers were rising, animated by the music, brushing off their wounds. Sharp stabs of bass coursed beneath colliding waves of synth with wraith-like vocals layered overtop, sighing for love.

I threw off the long sweeping train of my evening gown and replaced it with a cute, short little skirt covered in retro scale-mail accents that jangled when I walked. Since he didn't seem capable of dressing himself, I clothed Germanicus in a pair of dark blue jeans, tight-fitting, and a black t-shirt decorated by a silvery-winged angel with a scythe.

The dead began to dance. Overhead, the stars and the moon were replaced with shards of laser light. I pulled Germanicus deep into the dance, put my hands on his hips and pulled him close. My body was a marionette, the music its master.

He closed his eyes and put his hands on my shoulders. I could see that he was trying to fulfill his half of the bargain but he was rigid like a martyr impaled on a post.

"Relax," I ran my fingers in shiverring waves up and down his back. "Just move. Don't think."

He looked disoriented, sea-sick. Probably he'd had too much to drink.

"Lift me up," I told him finally. "I'll look for the way out."

He put his hands beneath my rib-cage and lifted me unto his shoulders. I could see the bodies surging out in every direction. Bodies in tandem. Bodies in motion. Bodies crashing against each other, moving apart, wave upon wave like fish in a net. They were beautiful. I craned my head back, arched my back and let the waves of disco-ball light wash over the curves of my dress.

"Well?" he asked.

"It goes on forever," I said. "Forever and ever. Beautiful bodies. Like molecules. Bouncing against each other. Building a world. Electrons. Protons. Opposites, drawn together by fate."

"Zombies," he declared. He pressed his palms against his temples, as if squeezing panic out. His breathing was heavy, and he reached towards his belt for a sword that wasn't there. "We've got to find a way out before they turn on us."

I could have stayed up there forever, but after another a minute Germanicus went down on one knee and helped me, rather gracelessly, to dismount. His paranoia had become stifling, and I could feel it rippling though the air. A breath of carnage wafted above the sweet scent of perfumed sweat, and a face turned towards us, hungry, its left eye gouged out.

He grabbed my hand and started dragging me through the crowd. It opened and parted, then closed tight around us. His other hand was stretched out like a cattle-prow in front of him as he pushed people aside.

Finally, he collided into something solid. A bar. I was sweating beautiful sweat, a sheen on my brow that caught every color of the neon rainbow flashing across the mirror behind the bar-tender. Germanicus ordered a double-vodka and knocked it back. At least it seemed to calm him down. I ordered a martini, and perched myself on one of the stools.

To the left was a door marked patio. So it wasn't infinite after all. I waited until Germanicus had ordered a second drink, and then pulled him along after me out into the open air.

We stepped across the threshold unto another plane. Worlds fell beneath us, pools of light where stars were being made, fantastic vistas of space where time itself was drowned in wondrous whirl-pools of darkness. I threw back my head and breathed in the strange, high-octane air of the place then took a sip of my drink. I felt like I could blow out my spirit like bubbles, like all of the stars were coming together to crowd about my hair. I was wonderful and I knew it. I reached out and craned my hand around the back of his neck. "Remember the dice toss?" I said. "You owe me a kiss."

He looked stunned, slightly stupefied, well overwhelmed. He knocked back his drink and tossed the glass away. Its thick bottom caught the light of nebulae as it spun out into space. His hand on my shoulder seemed almost like the hand of a drowning man grasping towards a lifeline. I pulled him close. Our lips met while worlds were born beneath our feet.

Farewell My Valentine

"Here we are," I whispered, leaning my head on his shoulder. "The last man and the last woman in the world. The last, and the first." I raised my head. My eyes were filled with the burst of newborn stars.

He stepped back, his eyes shut tight, the back of one of his hands rising to his lips. He drew it across them very slowly, as though my kiss were deeply ingrained dirt that was hard to wipe off. "I'm sorry," he said, his breathing ragged. "I should never have kissed you like that."

I climbed up onto the railing and leaned back, my hair trailing out into space. "Yes, you should. It's the only way. You understand it, instinctively. The only way out of this, for either of us, the only way to transcend death is to enter into love." My hand reached out to touch his cheek. It wasn't by any means an unlovable cheek, even if behind it there was a soul proud and bitter and full of violence. Maybe I could learn to love that soul for the sake of that cheek.

He looked up at me. For a moment, just a moment, he looked vulnerable, confused. "It's not that easy, Cataline."

"No one said it was." I paused. "For either of us."

He turned away, studying the dark reflections that we made on the door through which we'd come. "I mean I don't think it's possible. At least, it's not for me."

"Why not?"

A frustrated sigh. "Because every time I look at you, all that I can think about are the ways that you're not her."

He didn't even have the decency to hate me for myself. "I thought she wasn't your girlfriend."

"No. I was in love with her for years. But I was too proud to ever say."

I felt empty, erased by his regrets. "Seems like nothing's changed."

"How could it? There's no way to tell her now."

"I mean," a tight ball of fury wound itself up in my gut, "that she is not the only woman in the woman in the world. I mean that you have love and happiness right in front of you. But it's not good enough. Not for you. Because you're still so fucking proud."

"All right," he turned. "I'll play. You tell me this. What if I was ugly? A scrawny nerd with an overbite that could harbour ships? What if you couldn't turn me into your dreamboy just by changing my clothes? Would I be good enough for you?"

"I'm not completely shallow --"

"Oh yes you are. You just don't remember. You have no idea who you were, what you were like. But I do," he wore the same ugly love of triumph I'd seen when he'd gloated over the dead. "And I used to be that kid."

"So this is your revenge? For what? Because I hurt your little feelings when we were ten?"

"Revenge has nothing to do with it! Are you incapable of following an argument at all?"

"How am I supposed to follow anything when you're relying on things that I don't even know?" He opened his mouth, clearly about to enlighten me. I held up my hand. "No don't. Don't even tell me. I don't care." I turned away from him, gripping the balcony and staring out into the void. "I already know what you think of me. Shopping, clothes and boys. And you just love the fact that I don't remember enough to prove you wrong."

"I don't care if I'm wrong. That's not my point. My point is that I know for sure you don't love me. You love this face. That's all. It took extensive reconstructive surgery to make it look like this. Surgery I didn't want. And there is nothing I hate more than stupid, fatuous girls who teased me as a kid, and now they're madly in love with me because apparently I'm hot."

"That's not what this is about!" I gestured towards the distant space around us, the infinite expanses. "I'm not madly in love with you at all. I think you're rude. And proud. And cruel. But I also think you're the only one there is. And I'm smart enough to realize that means I have no choice."

"And shallow enough that you can't conceive of happiness unless it involves a boy."

I reached into my purse and fingered the pages of my diary. They seemed so brittle. A fragile manuscript. Fragments no longer bound together by their spine. "You think it's shallow," I said, "to want so badly just to love?"

"I think if you had any understanding of what love means, you'd understand why I can't just suddenly forget about Sheila and fall for you."

"Oh. Yes. I'm sure you understand so well. After all, you had some lame crush on a girl you never even told."

That silenced him. I took a step forward, intending to drive home my victory. I was stopped by the sound of something stirring beneath us in the deep. The monsters were rising, their bodies so black that they were invisible in the darkness. I could sense them even without sight, thrashing and panicked, packed in tight as bait-fish in a net. Looking up, I realized that they moved to the same rhythm as some wordless grief that passed behind his eyes.

We stood for a long time silent, listening to the drumbeat of our separate sorrows. At last, slowly, I reached out and took his hand. "I'm sorry. I didn't mean that." Far away, underneath the writhing black, there was an unseen flash. A distant cataclysm. A universe dying or being born. It might take a million years before the light reached us, before we could interpret what it meant. But we had that kind of time.